ON TROUBLESOME CREEK

BY THE SAME AUTHOR

NOVEL
River of Earth

POETRY
Hounds on the Mountain

James Still

ON TROUBLESOME CREEK

STORIES

FIRESIDE
INDUSTRIES

Published by Fireside Industries Books
An imprint of The University Press of Kentucky

Editorial and Sales Offices: The University Press of Kentucky
663 South Limestone Street, Lexington, Kentucky 40508-4008
www.kentuckypress.com

1941 edition published by Viking Press. Some of the material
in this volume first appeared as stories in *The American Mercury,*
Frontier and Midland, Mountain Life and Work, North Georgia Review,
Prairie Schooner, The Saturday Evening Post, Story, and *The Yale Review.*

Cataloging-in-Publication data for the 1941 edition is available from
the Library of Congress.

ISBN 978-1-950564-25-5 (pbk. : alk. paper)
ISBN 978-1-950564-26-2 (pdf)
ISBN 978-1-950564-27-9 (epub)

This book is printed on acid-free paper meeting
the requirements of the American National Standard
for Permanence in Paper for Printed Library Materials.

Manufactured in the United States of America

CONTENTS

I

Up-Creek

I Love My Rooster

WE LIVED in Houndshell mine camp the year of the coal boom, and I remember the mines worked three shifts a day. The conveyers barely ceased their rusty groaning for five months. I recollect the plenty there was, and the silver dollars rattling wherever men walked; and I recollect the goldfinches stayed that winter through, their yellow breasts turning mole-gray.

We were eating supper on a November evening when Sim Brannon, the foreman, came to tell Father of the boom. Word came that sudden. Father talked alone with Sim in the front room, coming back to the kitchen after a spell. A chuckle of joy broke in his throat as he sat down at the table again, swinging the baby off the floor onto his knee. He reached for the bowl of shucky beans, shaping a hill of them on his plate with a spoon. Never had he let us play with victuals. "They've tuck the peg off o' coal," he said. "Government's pulled the price tag. Coal will be selling hand over fist."

The baby stuck a finger into the bean mound. Father didn't scold. Mother lifted the coffeepot, shaking the spout clear of grounds. "I never heard tell it had a peg," she said.

Fern and Lark and I looked at Father, wondering what a coal peg was. The baby's face was bright and wise, as if he knew.

Father thumped the table, marking his words. "I say it's ontelling what a ton o' coal will sell for. They's a lack afar north at the big lakes, and in countries across the waters. I figure the price will double or treble." He lifted a hand over the baby's head. "Yon blue sky might be the limit."

Our heads turned toward the window. We saw only the night sky, dark as gob smoke.

Mother set the coffeepot down, for it began to tremble in her hand. She thrust a stick of wood into the stove, though supper was done and the room warm. "Will there be plenty in the camps?" she asked, uncertain.

Father laughed, spoon in air. "Best times ever hit this country," he said, jarring the table. "Why, I'm a-liable to draw twice the pay I get now." He paused, staring at us. We sat as under a charm, listening. "We're going to feed these chaps till they're fat as mud," he went on. "Going to put proper clothes on their backs and buy them a few pretties. We'll live like folks were born to live. This hard-scrabble skimping I'm tired of. We're going to fare well."

The baby made a cluck with his tongue, trying to talk. He squeezed a handful of beans until they popped between his fingers.

"For one thing," Father said, "I'm going to buy me a pair o' high-top boots. These clodhoppers I'm wearing have wore a half acre o' bark off my heels."

The cracked lids of the stove began to wink. Heat grew in the room.

"I want me a fact'ry dress," Fern spoke.

"I need me a shirt," I said. "A boughten shirt. And I want a game rooster. One that'll stand on my shoulder and crow."

Father glanced at me, suddenly angry.

"Me," Lark began, "I want—" But he could not think what he wanted most of all.

"A game rooster!" Father exclaimed. "They's too many gamble cocks in this camp already. Why, I'd a'soon buy you a pair o' dice and a card deck. I'd a'- soon."

"A pet rooster wouldn't harm a hair," I said, the words small and stubborn in my throat. And I thought of one-eyed Fedder Mott, who oft played mumbly-peg with me, and who went to the rooster matches at the Hack. Fedder would tell of the fights, his eye patch shaking, and I would wonder what there was behind the patch. I'd always longed to spy.

"No harm, as I see, in a pet chicken," Mother said.

"I want me a banty," Lark said.

Father grinned, his anger gone. He batted an eye at Mother. "We hain't going into the fowl business," he said. "That's for shore." He gave the baby a spoonful of beans. "While ago I smelled fish on Sim Brannon—fried salt fish he'd just et for supper. I'm a-mind to buy a whole wooden kit o' mackerel. We'll be able."

Mother raised the window a grain, yet it seemed no less hot. She sat down at the foot of the table. The baby jumped on Father's knee, reaching arms toward her. His lips rounded, quivering to speak. A bird sound came out of his mouth.

"I bet he wants a pretty-piece bought for him," Fern said.

"By juckers," Father said, "if they was a trinket would larn him to talk, I'd buy it." He balanced the baby in the palm of a hand and held him straight out, showing his strength. Then he keened his eyes at Mother. "You hain't said what you want. All's had their say except you."

Mother stared into her plate. She studied the wedge print there. She did not lift her eyes.

"Come riddle, come riddle," Father said impatiently.

"The thing I want hain't a sudden idea," Mother said quietly. Her voice seemed to come from a long way off. "My notion has followed me through all the coal camps we've lived in, a season here, a span there, forever moving. Allus I've aimed to have a house built on the acres we heired on Shoal Creek o'

Troublesome. Fifteen square acres we'd have to raise our chaps proper. Garden patches to grow victuals. Elbowroom a-plenty. Fair times and bad, we'd have a rooftree. Now, could we save half you make, we'd have enough money in time."

"Half?" Father questioned. "Why, we're going to start living like folks. Fitten clothes on our backs, food a body can enjoy." He shucked his coat, for he sat nearest the stove. He wiped sweat beads off his forehead.

"I need me a shirt," I said. "A store-bought shirt." More than a game rooster, more than anything, I wanted a shirt made like a man's. Being eight years old, I was ashamed to wear the ones Mother sewed without tails to stuff inside my breeches.

"No use living barebones in the midst o' plenty," Father said. "Half is too much."

Mother rose from the table and leaned over the stove. She looked inside to see if anything had been left to burn. She tilted the coffeepot, making sure it hadn't boiled dry. "Where there's a boom one place," she said, "there's bound to be a famine in another. Coal gone high, and folks not able to pay." Her lips trembled. "Fires gone out. Chaps chill and sick the world over withouten a roof above their heads." She picked up the poker, lifted a stove cap, and shook the embers. Drops of water began to fry on the stove. She was crying.

"Be-grabbies!" Father said. "Stop poking that fire! This room's already hot as a ginger mill."

ON A SATURDAY afternoon Father brought his two-week pay pocket home, the first since the boom. He came into the kitchen, holding it aloft, unopened. Mother was cooking a skillet of meal mush and the air was heavy with the good smell. I was in haste to eat and go, having promised Fedder Mott to meet him at the schoolhouse gate. Fedder and I planned to climb the mine tipple.

"Corn in the hopper and meal in the sack," Father said, rattling the pocket.

He let Fern and Lark push fingers against it, feeling the greenbacks inside; and he gave it to the baby to play with upon the floor, watching out of the tail of his eye. Mother was uneasy with Father's carelessness. The baby opened his mouth, clucking, churring. He made a sound like a wren setting a nest of eggs.

"Money, money," Fern said, trying to teach him.

He twisted his lips, his tongue straining. But he could not speak a word.

"I'd give every red cent to hear him say one thing," Father said.

The pay pocket was opened, the greenbacks spread upon the table. We had never seen such a bounty. Father began to figure slowly with fingers and lips. Fern counted swiftly. She could count nearly as fast as the Houndshell schoolteacher.

Father paused, watching Fern. "This chap can out-count a check-weigh-man," he bragged.

"Sixty-two dollars and thirty cents," Fern announced, and it was right, for Mother had counted too. "Wisht I had me a fact'ry dress," Fern said.

"I want a shirt hain't allus a-gaping at the top o' my breeches," I said.

Father wrinkled his forehead. "These chaps need clothes, I reckon. And I've got my fancy set on a pair o' boots. They's no use going about like raggle-taggle gypsies with money in hand. We're able to live decent."

"Socks and stockings I've knit," Mother said, "and shirts and dress garments I've sewed a-plenty for winter. They hain't made by store pattern, but they'll wear and keep a body warm. Now, I'm willing to do without and live hard to build a homeplace."

"Oh, I'm willing, too," Father complained, "but a man likes to get his grunt and groan in." He gathered the greenbacks, handing them to Mother. He stacked the three dimes. "Now, if I wasn't allus seeing the money, I could save without hurt. Once hit touches my sight and pocket, I'm afire. I burn to spend."

Mother rolled the bills. She thrust them into an empty draw sack, stowing all in her bosom. "One thing you could do," she told Father, "but it's not for me to say do, or not do. If you was a-mind, you could bring the pay pockets home unopened. We'd not think to save just half. I'd save all we could bear, spend what was needed. You'd not see the spark of a dime till we got enough for a house. I say this boom can't last eternal."

Father pulled his eyebrows, deciding. The baby watched. How like a bird he cocked his head. "Oh, I'm a-mind," Father said at last, "but the children ought to have a few coins to pleasure themselves with. A nickel a week."

"I want mine broke in pennies," Lark called.

Fern counted swiftly, speaking in dismay, "It would take me nigh a year to save enough for an ordered dress."

"We'll not lack comfort nor pleasure," Mother promised. "Nor will we waste. The chaps can have the nickel. You get a pair o' boots—a pair not too costy. And we'll buy a kit o' fish."

She stirred butter into the meal mush, and it was done. Fern hurried dishes upon the table.

"The pair my head was set on cost eighteen dollars. Got toes so sharp you could kick a blacksnake's eye out. Reckon I'll just make these clodbusters I got on do."

"Them boots must o' been sprigged with gold tacks."

A buttery steam rose from our plates. We dipped up spoonfuls of mush; we scraped our dishes, pushing them back for more.

"Hit's good to see no biled leather breeches on the table for once," Father said. He blew on a spoon of mush to cool it for the baby. "Right today I'll buy that kit o' fish."

"They're liable to draw every cat in Houndshell Holler. Better you plug the cat hole in the back door first."

I slid from the table bench, pulling my hat off a peg.

"Where are you traipsing to?" Father asked.

"Going to play with Fedder Mott. He's yonder in the schoolyard."

"I know Fedder Mott," Lark spoke, gulping mush. "He's a boy jist got one eyeball."

I ran the Houndshell road. A banjo twanged among the houses. A hundred smokes stirred in chimney pots, rising, threading chilly air. I reached the schoolhouse, breathing hard, and Fedder Mott was swinging on the gate. He jumped down.

"I'd nigh give you out," he said, his blue eye wide.

I said, "If my pap knowed about the tipple, I'd not got to come."

Fedder leaned against the fence. He was a full head taller than I, a year older. He drew a whack of tobacco from a hind pocket, bit a squirrely bite, and offered the cut to me.

I shook my head.

He puckered his lips, speaking around the wad in his jaw. "They hain't nothing worth seeing in that tipple tower. I done climbed thar." He waited, champing teeth into the wad, making juice to spit. "I'd figured we'd go to the rooster fight. Now you've come too late."

"Was I to go," I said, "my pap would tear up stakes."

Two children ran by, playing tag-o. A man came walking the road. Fedder spat into a rut. The black patch trembled on his face. It was like a great dark eye, dwarfing the blue one. I looked at it curiously.

"Afore long, fellers will be coming down from the Hack," Fedder said. "We'll larn which roosters whooped."

I studied the eye patch. It was the size of a silver dollar, hanging by a string looped around his head. What lay behind it? Was there a hole square into his skull? I was almost ashamed to ask, almost afraid. I drew a circle on the ground with my shoe toe, measuring the words: "I'll go to the rooster fight sometime, if one thing——"

"If'n what?"

"If you'll let me see your eye pocket."

Fedder blew the tobacco cud across the road. He pushed the long tails of his shirt inside his breeches. "You'll spy and won't go."

" 'F'ad die."

We saw a man walking the path off the ridge, coming toward us from the Hack. He came fast, though he was still too distant to be named. We watched him wind the crooked path and be lost among the houses.

"Ag'in' we go to the cockpit," Fedder said, "I'll let you look."

"I choose now."

Fedder stood firm. "Ag'in' that time, I will." He hushed a moment, listening for the man who came from the ridge. "Afore long I'll not be wearing this patch," he said. "I've heared o' glass eyeballs. Hit's truth. They say even a hound dog wears one in Anvers camp. Five round dollars they cost, and could I grab a holt on that much, I'd git the schoolteacher to mail an order."

"Won't your pap buy you a glass 'un?"

"If'n I was a flycatcher, he wouldn't feed me gnats."

"I'm going to save money, come every week. I've got me something in my head to buy."

"Hit reads in a magazine where a feller kin sell garden seeds and make a profit. A hundred packages o' squash and dill and turnip sold, and I'd have me enough."

We saw the man afar off on the road. He was heading our way, walking a hippety-hop on short legs.

"Bulger Hyden," Fedder said.

Fedder hailed him as he reached the schoolhouse gate, and he stopped. He shed his coat, being warm from haste, and he wore a green-dotted shirt.

"Who whooped?" Fedder asked.

Bulger Hyden's face grew wrinkled as a doty mushroom; he swung his arms emptily, glancing at the sky's promise of weather. There was a hint of snow. Goldfinches blew over us like leaves, piping their dry winter song above the conveyer's ceaseless rattle.

"Steph Harben's Red Pyle rimwrecked my Duckwing," Bulger grumbled. "Steph fotched that bird from West Virginia and scratches in all the money. I say it hain't fair pitting a furren cock." He folded his coat, balancing it on an elbow crotch, making ready to go. "I thought a sight o' my little Duckwing." His voice hoarsened. "I cherished that rooster." And he went on, and I looked after him, thinking a green-speckled shirt was the choicest garment ever a fellow could wear.

WINTER CAME BEFORE I could go to the Hack. Snow fell late in November and scarcely left the ground for two months. The rooster fights were halted until spring. I recollect the living river of wind pouring down Houndshell Hollow. For bird and varmint, and, I hear, for folk beyond the camps, it was a lean time. But miners fared well. I recollect the warm linsey coats, the red woolen gloves, the high-top boots; I recollect full pokes of food going into houses, and the smell of cooking victuals. Children wore store clothes. They bought spin-tops and pretties at the commissary. Boys' pockets clinked money. Only Fedder Mott and I had to wind our own balls and whittle our tops. I hoarded the nickels Mother gave me, telling Fedder I might buy a shirt when enough had been saved. Fedder never had a penny. He spoke bitterly of it. "My pap wouldn't plait me shucks if'n I was a chair bottom." And he said, "I hear tell hit's might' nigh the same with yore pap. Hit's told the eagle squalls when he looses a dollar."

Mother spent little. We hardly dared complain, having already more than we had known before. Once, in January, Father tried to figure the amount of money Mother had stored in the draw sack. He marked with a stub pencil, and Mother watched. At last he let the baby have the pencil. "My wage has riz three times," he said hopelessly, "though I don't know how much. Why, fellers tell me they're getting twelve and fifteen dollars a day. Deat Sheldon claims he made twenty dollars, four days hand-running, but he works a fold in the gravy tunnel and can load standing up."

"I've no idea o' the sum we've got," Mother said. "I opened one pay pocket and we're living out of it. The rest I've kept sealed."

"How's a body to know when a plenty's been saved? I hain't in a notion yet setting aside for tombstone and coffin box. Fellers in the mines 'gin to say the buffalo bellows when I spend a nickel."

"If you long for a thing enough, you'll give up for it. You'll sacrifice. The coal famine is bound to end some day. Come that time, we'll fit the house to the money."

Father began to tease. "What say we count the greenbacks? My curiosity is being et raw."

"Now, no. Hit would be a temptation to spend."

The baby sat up, threshing the air, puckering his lips. We looked, and he had bitten the rubber tip off the pencil.

"Hain't he old enough to be saying words?" Father asked.

"He talked to a cat once," Lark said. "I heared him."

"Ah, now," Mother chided. "Just a sound he made. Cats follow stealing in since we bought salt fish. Can't keep the cat hole plugged."

"He said 'kigid.' "

"That hain't a word," Fern said.

Father poked a finger at the baby. "By gollyard, if he'd just speak one word!"

The baby lifted his arms, mouth wide, neck stretched. He crowed.

"Thar's your rooster," Father chuckled, setting his eyes on me.

"I aim to own a real gamer," I bragged, irked by Father's teasing. "I aim to." I spoke without hope, not knowing that by spring it would come true.

"A good thing to have this double zero weather," Father drawled. "Hit driv the poker players and fowl gamblers indoors. But fellers claim that when the weather mends they'll be rooster fights in the Hack three days a week. Hit's high-low-jack and them fools lose every button cent."

Mother searched the baby's mouth for the pencil tip. "I call this boom a gamble," she said. "It's bound to end." She didn't find the rubber tip, for the baby had swallowed it down.

I told Fedder of Mother's prophecy as we sat by a fire on the creek bank. We had fish-hooks in an ice hole.

"Be-hopes the boom lasts till I git me a glass eye," he said. "My mind's set on it. I'd better have a batch o' garden seeds ordered and start selling."

"You couldn't stick a pickax in the ground, it's so froze," I told him. "Folks haven't a notion to buy seeds now."

Fedder rubbed his hands over the blaze, blowing a foggy breath. "I say winter hain't going to last forever neither."

I recollect thinking the long cold spell would never end. January diddled, and February crawled. March warmed a bit, thawing. The breasts of goldfinches turned yellow as rubbed gold again. Fedder got his seeds, though when he should have been peddling them he'd climb the ridge to the rooster fights. Oft when a rooster was killed they'd let him bring the dead fowl home. Father forbade my going to the Hack; he put his foot down. But next to seeing was Fedder's telling. I came to know the names of the bravest cocks. I knew their markings, and the way they fought.

Fedder whistled for me one Thursday evening at the edge of dark. I heard and went outside, knowing his Kentucky redbird call. He stood beyond the fence with a coffee sack bundled in his arms; and he seemed fearful and anxious, and yet proud. His blue eye was wide, and the black patch had a living look. Packages of seeds rattled in his pockets.

"How much money have you mized?" he asked. "How much?" His voice was a husky whisper.

I guessed what the bundle held, scarcely daring to believe. I grew feverish with wonder.

"Eleven nickels," I said. "I couldn't save all."

The coffee sack moved; something threshed inside. A fowl's wings struck its thighs.

"I'm a-mind to sell you half ownership in my rooster," he said. "I will for yore eleven nickels, and if you'll keep him till I find a place. My pap would wring hits neck if I tuck him home."

I touched the bundle. My hand trembled. I shook with joy. "I been saving to buy a shirt," I said. "I want me a boughten shirt."

"You couldn't save enough by Kingdom Come. Eleven nickels, and jist you pen him. We'll halvers."

"Who'd he belong to?"

"Fotch the money. All's got to be helt a secret."

I brought my tobacco-sack bank and Father's mine lamp. We stole under the house, penning the rooster in a hen-coop.

Father's voice droned over us in the kitchen. Fedder lit the lamp to count the money. The rooster stood blinking, red-eyed, alert. His shoulders were white, redding at the wing bows. Blood beads tipped his hackle feathers. His spurs were trimmed to fit gaffs. It was Steph Harben's Red Pyle.

"How'd you come by him?" I insisted.

"He fit Ebo, the black Cuban, and got stumped. He keeled down. They was a cut on his throat and you'd a-thought him knob dead. Steph give him to me, and ere I reached the camp, he come alive. That thar cut was jist a scratch."

We crawled from beneath the house. Fedder smothered the light. "Don't breathe this to a soul," he warned. "Steph would auger to git him back, and my pap would throw duck fits. Now, you bring him to the schoolhouse ag'in' two o'clock tomorrow."

He moved toward the gate, the nickels ringing in his pocket. I went into the house and sat quietly behind the stove, feeling lost without my money, though recompensed by the rooster.

Father spoke, trotting the baby to Burnham Bright on a foot. "Warm weather's come," he mused. "Seems to me the Hound-shell company ought to pare down on mining. Two days ago they hired four new miners, fellers from away yander."

"I know a boy come from Alabamy," Lark said. "I bet he's from yon side the waters."

"It's United States, America," Fern said.

"Sim Brannon believes something's bound to crack before long," Father went on. "Says hit's liable to come sudden. I'm in hopes my job don't split off."

"Come that time," Mother said, "maybe we'll have plenty saved for a house."

Father reached the baby to Mother. "I'm going to bed early," he yawned. "Last night I never got sixty winkles o' sleep. I reckon every tomcat in this camp was miaowing on the back porch."

"The fish draws 'um."

"A tinker man tapped on the door yesterday," Fern said, "and a big nanny cat ran in betwixt his legs."

"Hit's the one baby talked a word to," Lark said.

Father stretched sleepily. "I'm afeared the baby's a mute," he said. He set his chair aside. "The only thing that'd keep me awake this night would be counting the money we've got stacked away."

I WAITED AT the schoolhouse gate, holding the rooster by the shanks. He snuggled against my jump jacket, pecking at the buttons. He stuck his head in my jacket pocket to see what was there. After a spell Fedder came, his eye patch trembling and the garden seeds as noisy upon him as grass crickets.

"Why'n't you kiver him?" he asked crossly. "He might a-been seen."

"He flopped the coffee sack off," I said. "Anyhow, he's been seen already. Crowed this morning before blue daylight and woke my pap. If I hadn't cried like gall, he'd been killed. Now it's your turn to keep."

Fedder bit a chew of tobacco, bit it with long front teeth as a squirrel bites. He spat into the road and looked up and down. "If I tuck him to my house, he'd be in the skillet by dinner." He closed his eye to think, and there was only the black patch staring. "Reckon we'll have to sell him," he said presently. "I figure Steph Harben will buy him back. He's yon side the commissary, playing draughts. Air you of a notion?"

The cock lifted his head, poising it left and right. I loosed my hold about his legs and stroked his bright saddle. He sat on my arm.

"This rooster's a pet," I said. "When I tuck him out o' the coop, he jumped square onto my shoulder and crowed. I'm taking a liking to him."

"I jist lack selling fourteen seed papers gitting my eyeball. Never could I sell dills and rutabagas. If Steph will buy the rest, I'll rid my part. We got nowheres earthy to store a chicken."

"I hain't a-mind to sell."

Fedder packed the ground where he stood. The seeds rattled. The rooster pricked his head.

"You stay here till I git Steph," Fedder said. He swung around. "You stay."

He went in haste, and suddenly a great silence fell in the camp. The coal conveyer at the mines had stopped. Men stood at the drift mouth and looked down upon the rooftops. It was so still I could hear the far *per-chic-o-ree* of finches. I held the rooster at arm's length, wishing him free as a bird. I half hoped he would fly away. I set him on the fence, but he hopped to my shoulder and shook his wattles.

Back along the road came Fedder. Steph Harben hastened with him, wearing a shirt like striped candy, and never a man wore a finer one. The shirt was thinny—so thin that when he stood before me I could see the paddles of his collarbones.

Fedder said, "I've sold my part. Hit's you two trading."

Steph said, "Name yore price. Name."

I gathered the fowl in my arms. "I hain't a-mind to sell," I said.

We turned to stare at miners passing, going home long before quitting time, their cap lamps burning in broad day.

Steph was anxious. "Why hain't you willing?" he asked. "Name."

I dug my toe into the ground, scuffing dirt. "I love my rooster," I said. But I looked up at Steph's shirt. It was very beautiful.

"If'n you'll sell," Fedder promised, "I'll let you spy at my eye pocket. Now, while it's thar, you kin look. Afore long I'll have a glass 'un."

I kicked a clod into the road. "I'll swap my part o' the rooster for that striped shirt. It can be cut down to fit."

"Shuck it off," Fedder told Steph.

Steph unbuttoned the shirt, slipped it over the blades of his shoulders, and handed it to me in a wad. He snatched the rooster, lighting out for home, and miners along the road glared at his bare back.

Fedder brushed his hat aside, catching the eye patch between forefinger and thumb. I was suddenly afraid, suddenly having no wish to see.

The patch was lifted. I looked, stepping back, squeezing the shirt into a ball. I turned, running, running with this sight burnt upon my mind.

I ran all the way home, going into the kitchen door as Father went, not staying the sow cat that stole in between my legs. Mother sat at the table, a pile of greenbacks before her, the empty pay pockets crumpled.

"Hell's bangers!" Father gasped, dropping heavily upon a chair and lifting the baby to his knee; and when he could speak above his wonder, "The boom's busted. I've got no job." But he laughed, and Mother smiled.

"I've heard already," Mother said. She laid a hand upon the money bills, flicking them under a thumb like a deck of gamble cards. "There's enough here to build a house, a house with windows looking out o' every room. And a grain left for a pair o' costy boots, a boughten shirt, a fact'ry dress, a few pretties."

The baby opened his mouth, curling his lips, pointing a stub finger. He pointed at the old nanny smelling the fish kit.

"Cat!" he said, big as life.

The Proud Walkers

WE MOVED out of Houndshell mine camp in May to the home-place Father had built on Shoal Creek, and I recollect foxgrapes were blooming and there was a spring chill in the air. Fern and Lark and I ran ahead of the wagon, frightening water thrushes, shouting back at the poky mare. We broke cowcumber branches to wave at the baby, wanting to call to him, but he did not then have a name.

Only Mother forbore stretching eyes to see afar. She held the baby atop a shuck tick, her face pale with dread to look upon the house. A mort of things she had told Father before he had gone to raise the dwelling. "Ere a board is rived," she'd said, "dig a cellar. There'll be no more pokes o' victuals coming from the commissary." She had told him the pattern for the chimney, roof, and walls; she told him more than a body could keep in his head, saying at last, "Could I lend a hand, 'twould be a satisfaction."

Father had grinned. "A nail you drove would turn corkscrew A blow-sarpent couldn't quile to your saw marks. Hit's man's work. A man's got to wear the breeches." Oh, Father nearly had a laughing spell listening to Mother's talk. Mother had said, "A house proper to raise chaps in, a cellar for laying by food, and lasty neighbors. Now, that hain't asking for the moon-ball."

I recollect bull-bats soared overhead when we reached Shoal Creek in the late afternoon; I recollect Mother looked at the house, and all she had feared was true. The building stood windowless, board ends of walls were unsawn, and the chimney pot barely cleared the hip-roof. But Fern and Lark and I were awed. We could not think why Mother dabbed her eyes with baby's dress tail.

"Hit's not finished to a square T," Father said uneasily. "After planting they'll be time in plenty. A late start I've got. Why, field corn and a garden ought to be breaking ground. Just taste a grain o' patience."

Mother glanced into the sky where bull-bats hawked. She was heartsick with the mulligrubs. Her voice sounded tight and strange. "A man's notions are ontelling," she said, "but if this creek's a fitten place to bring up chaps, if good neighbors live nigh, reckon I've got no right to complain."

"The Crownover family lives yon side the ridge," Father said. "Only folks in handy walking distance. I hear they're the earth's salt. No needcessity o' lock or key on Shoal Creek."

The wagon was unloaded by dusk dark. Father lighted the lamp on coming from stabling the mare, and we hovered to a smidgen of fire. We trembled in the night chill, for it was foxgrape winter. Mother feared to heap wood on the blaze, the chimney pot being low enough to set sparks to the roof. She knelt by the hearth, frying a skillet of hominy, cooking it mortal slow.

Father saddled the baby on a knee. "Well, now," he said, buttoning his jump jacket and peeping to see what the skillet held, "reckon I've caught a glimpse o' neighbors already. I heard footsteps yon side the barn in a brushy draw, though I couldn't see for blackness till they'd topped the ridge. There walked two fellers, with heads size o' washpots."

Lark crept nearer Mother. Fern and I glanced behind us. Nailheads shone on the walls as bright as the eyes of beasts.

"I figure it to be men carrying churns or jugs on their shoulders," Mother spoke coldly.

"I saw a water-head baby in the camps once," Fern said. "I did."

"Hit might a-been Old Bloody Tom and some-'un," Lark said.

"Odd they'd go by our place," Father mused, "traveling no path." He joggled the baby on his knee, making him squeal. "But it's said them Crownovers can be trusted to Jordan River and back ag'in. I'm wanting to get acquainted the first chance."

"A man's fancy to take short cuts," Mother replied, nodding her head at the boxed room. "They're men cutting across from one place to another, taking the lazy trail."

Fern's teeth chattered. She was ever the scary one.

"I hain't a chip afraid," I bragged, rashy with curiosity. "Be they boys amongst them Crownovers? I'm a-mind to play with one."

"Gee-o," Father chuckled, "a whole bee swarm o' chaps. Stair-steppers, creepers, and climbers, biddy ones to nigh growns. Fourteen, by honest count. A sawyer at Beddo Tillett's mill says they all can whoop weeds out of a crop in one day."

"I be not to play with water-heads," Lark said.

"That sawyer says every one o' Izard Crownover's young 'uns have rhymy names," Father went on. "He spun me a few, many as he could think of. Bard, Nard, Dard, Guard, Shard—names so slick yore tongue trips up."

"Are there girls too?" Fern asked.

"Beulah, Dulah, Eulah. A string like that."

Mother stirred the hominy. "Clever neighbors I've allus wanted," she said, her voice gloomy, "and allus I've longed for a house fitten to make them welcome."

"Be-jibs!" Father spoke impatiently. "A fair homeseat we'll have once the crop's planted, and they's a spare minute. Why, I raised this place off the ground in twelve days, elbow for axle.

I didn't have half the proper tools; I had no help-hands. I hauled lumber twelve miles from Beddo Tillett's sawmill." He grunted, untangling baby's fingers from his watch chain. "Anyhow, hit might take them Crownovers a year's thawing to visit. Hain't like the camps where folks stick noses in, the first thing. I say let time get in its lick."

We were quieted by the thought of enduring a lonesome year, of nobody coming to put his feet under our table, nobody to borrow, or heave and set and calculate weather. Oh, the camps had spoiled us with their slew of chaps and rattling coal conveyers and people's talky-talk. Dwelling there, you couldn't stretch your elbows without hitting people.

I said, sticking my lips out, "I hain't waiting till I'm crookback ere I play with some'un."

Fern batted her eyes, trying to cry. "Ruther to live on a gob heap than where no girls are."

The skillet jiggled in Mother's hand. She spoke, complaining of the house, though now it was small in her mind compared with this new anxiety. "Nary a window cut," she said. "A house blind as a mole varmint."

"Jonah's whale!" Father exclaimed angrily. His ears reddened. He galloped his knee. "A feller can't whittle windowframes with a pocket knife. I reckon nothing will do but I hie at daybreak to Tillett's and 'gin making them. Two days it'll take; two I ought to be rattling clods. Why, a week's grubbing to be done before a furrow's lined. Crops won't mature planted so late." He swallowed a great breath. "Had we the finest cellar in Amerikee, a particle o' nothing there'd be for winter storing."

"I reckon I've set my bonnet too high," Mother admitted. "The cellar's got to be filled with canning, turnips, cabbages, and pickling, if we're to eat the year through. Now, windows can be put off, but the chimley's bound to have a taller stacking."

The blood hasted from Father's ears. Never could he stay angry long. He coaxed baby to latch hands on his lifted arm and swing. "Ought to fill the new barn loft so full o' corn and fodder hits tongue will hang out," he said. He taught the baby to skin a cat, come-Andy-over, head foremost. "One thing besides frames I'm fotching, and that's a name for this tadwhacker. Long enough he's gone without."

"Hain't going to call him Beddo," Fern said. "That's the ugliest name-word ever was."

"Not to be Tillett neither," Lark said.

The hominy browned. We held plates in our laps. The yellow kernels steamed a mellow smell. It was hard not to gobble them down like an old craney crow.

Mother ate a bit, then sat watching Father. "I had a house pattern in my head," she said, "and I ached to help build, to try my hand making it according. And I'd wished for good neighbors. But house and neighbors hain't a circumstance to getting a crop and the garden planted. Hit's back to the mines for us if we don't make victuals. Them windowframes can wait."

"I can't follow a woman's notions," Father said. "For peace o' mind I'd better gamble two days and get the windows in." He chuckled, his mouth crammed. "I'd give a Tennessee pearl to see you atop a twenty-foot ladder potting nails." His chuckle grew to laughter; it caught like a wind in his chest, blowing out in gusts, shaking him. He began to cough. A kernel had got in his windpipe. His jaws turned beety; he sneezed a great sneeze. We struck our doubled fists against his back, and presently the grain was dislodged. "Ah, ho," he said, swallowing, "had I a-died, 'twould been in good cause."

Mother lightened. "I'm no witty with a hammer and saw," she said, "and if that cellar's not dug to my fancy, I can spade."

Father sobered. He got as restless in his chair as a caged bird. Of a sudden he turned his head to the door, listening. "Hush-o!" he said. We pricked our ears. "Hush!"

We waited, unbreathing, hearing the harsh *peent* of bull-bats.

"I heard nothing onnatural," Mother said.

Fern shivered. Lark searched under the beds. He knew boogers were abroad at night.

Father reached the baby to Mother, and got up. So sleepy baby was, his head rolled like a dropped gourd. "The mare's restless," Father decided. "She might o' heard Crownover's stally bray yon side the mountain. I'll see that she's latched in tight." He went outside.

"Let's play Old Bloody Tom," Lark said. "I be Tom, a-rambling, smoking my pipe. You all be sheeps."

"Now, no," Fern snuffed. "It'd make me scared."

We children were abed when Father returned. He shucked off his boots and dabbed tallow on them; he breathed on the leather and rubbed it fiercely with a linsey rag. He spoke, faltering, hunting words, "I've been aiming to tell about the cellar."

Mother fitted a skillet's eye to a peg. She paused.

"After I'd shingled the roof," Father said, "I put in to dig. Got three feet down and struck bottom. This house is setting on living rock. I've larnt they hain't a cellar on Shoal Creek. This vein runs under all."

And later, when the light was blown, I heard Father speak from his pillow. "I saw more fellers on the ridge a while ago, walking with heads so square I figured they hefted boxes on their shoulders. I'm a-mind to stop by the Crownovers' tomorrow, asking a hinting question. Hit's quare folks would go a dark way no road treads."

The sun-ball was eating creek fog when Mother waked me. The door stood wide upon morning. "Your father's gone to Tillett's already," she said, "and against my will and beg. He hurried off afoot, saying he'd let the mare rest, saying he'd get the window-frames hauled somehow." She gazed dolesomely upon the fields where blackgum, sassafras, and redbud grew as in a young forest. "I argued, I plead, yet he would to go. Oh, man-judgment's like weather. Hit's onknowing."

My breeches were on in a wink. I'd thought to go feed the mare, then hie to the brushy draw to quest for signs of walkers. I went before eating, being more curious than hungry. I fed the mare ten ears of corn; I stole beyond the barn. The draw was a moggy place. Wahoos grew thick against a limerock wall, and a sprangle of water ran out. I found a nest of brogan tracks set in the mud; I saw where they printed the ridge. "If I was growed up," I spoke aloud, "I'd follow them steps, be they go to the world's end." Then I ran to the house; I ran so fast a bluesnake racer couldn't have caught me.

Mother was putting dough bread and rashers on the table when I hurried indoors. Her face was gaunt with worry. She circled the table where Fern and Lark ate. Baby threshed in his tall chair, sucking a meat rind. "It would take Adam's grands and greats to rid that ground in time for planting," she said. "I tried grubbing a pawpaw, but its roots sunk to Chiney. I'm afeared we might have to backtrack to the mines. We'll be bound to, if the crops don't bear."

"I've seen a quare thing," I said.

Mother paid me no mind. "Two days your father will be gone, and no satisfaction I'll see till he returns. Yet he can't grub by his lone. He'd not get through in time." She halted, staring at the walls, searching in her head for what to do.

"Never was a mine shack darker," she said at last, having decided. She rolled her sleeves above her elbows, like a man's. "I can't grub fitten. I can't dig a cellar through puore rock. But window holes I can saw—holes three feet by five." She fetched a hatchet and a handsaw; she marked a window by tape.

"I'd be scared of a night, with holes cut," Fern complained. "Robber men might come."

"I saw tracks," I blurted. My words were drowned under Mother's chopping. She hewed a crevice to give the sawblade lee.

"It's Father's work," Fern whined. She squeezed her eyelids, trying to cry.

I recollect Mother worked that day through, cutting four windows, true as a sawyer's. The hours crawled turkle-slow. Fern and Lark and I longed for shouting children; we longed for the busy noises of the camps. We could only mope and look at the empty road. Nobody passed up-creek or down, nobody we glimpsed from daybreak to dusk dark. Oft when Mother took a little rest she'd glance the hills over. Oh, she was lost as anyone. Loneliness swelled large as mast-balls inside of us.

When night came we heard the first lorn cry of a chuck-will's-widow. The evening chill was sharp. We ate supper huddled to a mite of fire. "One spark against a shingle," Mother explained, "and we'd have to roust a fox from his cave house. That chimley begs fixing."

The dishes were washed and put away. We sat quietly, our faces yellow in the lamplight. The *peent* of bull-bats came through the window holes. Spring lizards prayed for rain in the bottoms.

Mother saw how our eyes kept stealing to the window. The darkness there was black as corpse cloth. "Sing a ballad or play a game," she urged. "Then hap baby will go to sleep."

"Play Bloody Tom," Lark called. "I be Tom, coming for a coal to tetch my pipe. You be sheeps or chaps."

"Now, no," Fern said, "that 'un's scary."

"Let's do a talking song," I chose. "Let's sing 'Old Rachel,' and me do the talking."

We sang "Old Rachel"; Old Rachel nobody could do a thing with; Old Rachel going to the Bad Place with her toenails dragging and a bucket on her arm, saying, "Good morning, Mister Devil, hit's getting mighty warm"; and I spoke, after every verse, "Now, listen, Little Rachel, please be kind o' quiet."

We hushed suddenly. Beast sounds rang the hills. Crownover's stallion had trumpeted afar, and our mare had whinnied.

"Sing ahead," Mother coaxed, "the mare's stall is latched. I saw to it. Sing what the Devil done with Rachel when he couldn't handle her."

We had no heart to sing more. "I propped the stall door," I said. Fern's eyes were beaded upon the black window. "Wisht it was allus day," she said.

"Ah, now," Mother chided, trying to comfort us. "A body gets their growth of a night. I'd not want the baby a dwarf."

"I saw a low-standing man in the camps once," Fern recalled, "not nigh tall as me."

"I saw tracks in the draw—" I began, and hushed. They grew in my mind. They seemed to have been made by the largest foot a man ever had. The thought held my breath. "Wisht Poppy was here," I said.

The baby sat up, round-eyed, blinking.

Mother spoke, making talk. "I wonder what name your father's going to bring this chap. I promised him the naming."

"He'll fotch a sour 'un," Fern grudged. "Ooge, Boll, Zee. One like smut-face little 'uns wear at the mines."

"I told your father, 'Name him for an upstanding man. A man clever, with heart and pride.'"

"Hope it's a rhymer," I said. "Whoever named them fourteen Crownovers was clever. Hit tuck a head full o' sense to figure all o' them."

"Once I knew a man who had a passel o' children," Mother related. "He married two times and pappyed twenty-three. After there come sixteen, he ran out o' names. Just called them numbers, according to order. Seventeen, eighteen, nineteen, twenty—" She paused, watching baby. He slept, leant upon nothing, like a beast sleeps.

"If Poppy was here," Fern yawned, "I bet he'd laugh."

"You'll all be dozing on foot before long," Mother told us. "Time to pinch the wick."

The lamp was smothered; we crawled between covers. Once the light died the window hole turned gray. You could see the shoulders of hills through it. Fern and Lark hushed and slept. I lay quiet, listening, and my ears were large with dark, catching midges of sound. The shuck mattress ticked, ticked, ticked. A rooster crowed. Night wore.

In my sleep I heard the mare thresh in her stall, pawing the ground with a forefoot. I raised on an elbow. From behind the barn came an owly cough, and a voice saying, "Hold!" Someone stood inside the window, tall, white-gowned. It was Mother. I sprang beside her, looking. Fellows topped the ridge as ants march, up and over. Their heads were like folks' heads, but their backs were humpty.

"Six walkers with pokes," Mother said, "carrying only God knows what."

I RECOLLECT WAKING with the sun in my face; I recollect thinking Father would come home that day, bringing the frames to set against robbers and bloom winters. Lark was asleep beside me, and Fern and the baby lay in Mother's bed with their heads on a duck pillow. I recollect glancing through the window and seeing Mother run out of the fields.

I stood in my shirttail as Mother swung the door. Her hair fell wild about her shoulders. For a moment she had no breath to speak. "The mare's gone!" she gasped. "Gone."

Fern roused, meany for being awakened with a start. Lark's eyes opened, damp and large.

"I propped the stall door," I vowed. "Hit was latched and propped too."

"Had Poppy been at home," Fern quarreled, "stealers wouldn't a-come."

"I'd have figured she broke the latch of her own free will," Mother said, "hadn't it been for where the tracks led. I followed."

"Was they brogan prints alongside?" I asked. They grew immense in my mind. "Bigger'n anything?"

"Just bare mare tracks. I followed within sight o' the Crownovers.'"

Of a sudden I scorned the Crownovers. I could hear blood drum my ears. I said, "If I met one o' them chaps, I'd not know him from dirt. I'd not speak a howdy."

Fern twisted into her garments. "I bet them girl-chaps wear old flour-sack dresses, and you kin read print front and back." She wrinkled her nose, making to cry. "I'm wanting to move to Houndshell." She flicked her eyelids, but not a tear would come. She got angry, angry as I. "Ruther be dust in a grave box than have to do with them folks. Be my name theirs, I couldn't hold up my head for shame."

"Don't lay blame for shore," Mother warned. "The mare's tracks went straight, yet they might o' veered a bit this side. There's nothing we can settle till your father's here, and he aimed to stop by Crownovers' anyhow."

Fern stamped her feet against the floor. "I wisht this house would burn to ashes. We'd be bound to live at the mines where they's girls to play with, and hain't no robbers."

"Ramshack house, a-setting on a rock," I mocked.

Mother turned hurt eyes upon us. She stood before the cold fireplace and began to lay off with hands like the Houndshell schoolteacher. "Fifteen years we lived under a rented roof, fifteen years o' eating out o' paper pokes. We were beholden to the mines, robbed o' fresh breathing air, robbed o' green victuals. Now, cellar nor neighbors we've got here, but there's clean air and ground and home. I say this house hain't going to burn. That chimley's to rise higher."

"Poppy ought to be a-coming," Lark sniffled.

"The land not grubbed," Mother lamented, "no seeds planted, the mare stolen. Oh, it's Houndshell for us another winter." She turned away, her shoulders drawn and small.

We children ate breakfast alone, one of us forever peering through the window hole toward the way Father would come. Fern held the baby, giving him tastes of mush. We scraped the pot; we sopped our plates, for Mother had gone into the far room. But she came as we pushed the chairs aside. We stared. She wore Father's breeches. The legs were rolled at the bottom. "I can't climb a ladder or straddle a roof in a dress," she said. "Allus I've wanted to take a hand with this house. Here's my chance, before your father's back. He'd tear up the patch if he knew."

"It's man's work," Fern said grumpily.

Rocks were gathered, clay batter stirred, a ladder leaned against the roof. Up Mother went with a bucket of mud. I climbed, lifting the rocks in a coffee sack, reaching the poke's neck to her on gaining the tiptop. Mother edged along the hip-roof, balancing the sack and bucket. Her face went dead white. Traveling the steep of a roof was not as simple as spoken.

Fern began to whimper, and the baby cried a spasm. "Come down!" Fern called. "Come down!"

Mother buttered two rocks with clay, placing them on the chimney. They rolled off, falling inside. She was slapping mud to a third when a voice roared beside the house. A man stood agape. A stranger had come unbeknownst. Mother jerked, and the bucket slipped, and the coffee sack emptied in a clatter across the shingles. The fellow had to jump limber dodging that rock fall. He roared, laughing, "Come down, woman, afore you break yore neck!" Mother obeyed, red-faced, ashamed of the breeches she wore.

We studied the man. He was older than Father, smaller, and two hands shorter. His eyes were bright as new tenpennies. An empty pipe stuck out of his mouth, the bowl a tiny piggin carved from an oak boss. "When a woman undertakes man's gin-work," he spoke, "their fingers all turn to thumbs." He didn't stand back. He hauled rocks and a new batch of clay up the ladder; he fashioned that chimney to a fare-you-well.

Lark and Fern and I whispered together.

Fern asked, "Who be this feller?"

Lark ventured, "Hit might be Old Bloody Tom, come for a coal o' fire."

I mouthed words in their ears. "I'd vow he's not a Crownover. His feet hain't big enough."

"We're obliged," Mother said when the stranger descended. She wore a dress now, though she was still abashed.

The man bowed his arms, tipped the pipe, discounting. "A high perch I've needed to search about. A horse o' mine broke stable last night. I'm looking for him."

Lark raised on his toes, straining to tell of our mare. Mother hushed him with a glance.

"Animals are apt to go traipsing with another nigh," the man continued, eying the barn, "but they usually come home by feeding time. Like as not, they'll bring in a furren critter, and it's a puzzle to whom they're belongen. I allus said, men and beast air cut from the same ham." He bent his knees to glance under the house, and grunted knowingly. He shuffled to go. "Yonder atop the roof I beheld you've got a sight o' grubbing to do. Hit'd take Methuselum's begats to ready that ground for seed." He started off, speaking over his shoulder, "If you had fitten neighbors, they'd not fail to help." He went down-hill and up-creek, and we watched him out of sight.

We set a steady lookout for Father. As the hours crept into afternoon Mother complained, her voice at the rag edge of patience, "Your father ought to come while daylight's burning."

But Father arrived when the bull-bats were flying and night darkened the hollows, and he came alone and empty-handed. No windowframes he brought. I recollect he smiled on seeing our glum faces in the light of the great fire Mother had built. Even baby sulled a mite.

"What bush did you get them pouts off of?" he asked.

Mother lifted her hands in defeat. "I'm a-mind we'll have to endure the camps a spell longer."

"Hark!" Father exclaimed. How strangely he looked at Mother, at us all. The mulligrubs were writ deep upon our faces.

"The mare stolen, no chance for a crop. Oh, the sorriest of folks we've moved nigh."

"Hark-o!"

"Them Crownovers hain't fitten neighbors," Fern scoffed, "A man come a-saying it."

I spoke with scorn, "They've got rhymy chaps. Their names sound like an old raincrow hollering '*cu cu cu, cucucu.*'"

"A man come a-saying——"

"Even if the garden and crop were planted," Mother despaired, "there'd be no place earthy to store winter food."

Father grinned. "Why, we've got a cellar dug by the Man Above. Old Izard Crownover says it's yonder in that brushy draw—a cave hole in solid lime-rock that'll keep stuff till Glory. Now he ought to know."

Our mouths fell open. We could scarcely believe.

"Ah, ho," Father chortled, swinging the baby onto his shoulder. "They's another thing we've got for sartin, and that's a name for this little tadwhacker. He's to be named for a feller proud as ever walked. I'm going to call him Zard, after Old Izard."

"A man come a-saying——"

"Old Izard himself," Father said. "Why, them Crownovers are so proud they dreaded telling us o' using our cave for a cellar. They called hit trespassing. Walked their stuff out in the black o' night,"

"The mare might o' broke the latch," Mother admitted, "but her tracks went straight as a measure."

"Come morning," Father chuckled, "you kin look up Shoal Creek, and there'll be the mare and Crownover's stally hauling windowframes in a wagon. And there'll be Old Izard and his woman and all his rhymers a-walking, coming to help grub, plow, and seed. Such an ant bed o' folks you'll swear hit's Coxey's Army."

Father halted, remembering what Izard had told him. He eyed Mother and began to laugh. Laughter boiled inside of him. He could barely make words, so balled his tongue was. "From now on," he gulped, "thar's one thing for shore." He threshed the air, his face fiery with joy. "I'm the one wearing the breeches." He struggled for breath. He choked.

Mother struck the flat of her hands against his back. "The nature of a man is a quare thing," she said.

Locust Summer

I RECOLLECT the June the medicine drummer and his woman came down Shoal Creek and camped three days in our mill. That was the summer of Mother's long puny spell after the girl-baby was born; it was the time seventeen-year locusts cried "Pharaoh" upon the hills, and branches of oak and hickory perished where their waxy pins of eggs were laid. Wild fruit dried to seeds, and scarcely would birds peck them, so full their crops were with nymphs. Mulberries in the tree behind our house ripened untouched. Lark and I dared not taste, fearing to swallow a grub. Fern vowed not to eat, though I remember her tongue stayed purple till dog days.

"A rattlesnake's less pizenous than berries in a locust season," Mother kept warning. She knew our hunger; she knew how sorry Father's cooking was. "A body darst eat off o' vine or tree."

"A reg'lar varmint and critter year," Father told Mother. "Aye gonnies, if they hain't nigh as many polecats in the barn as they's locust amongst trees. Yet nothing runs as wild as these chaps. Clothes a puore tear-patch, hands rusty as hinges. Hit'll be a satisfaction when you're able to take them back under your thumb. I'd a'soon tend a nest o' foxes."

"I figure to strengthen when the locusts hush," Mother said. "A few more days o' roaring and they'll be gone." And she glanced at Fern, being most worried about her. "Still, I can't make a child take pride if they're not born with it. Fern's hair is matty as a brush heap. It's eating her eyes out."

"Humph," Fern said. She didn't care a mite.

Lark and I would look scornfully at the baby nestled in the crook of Mother's arm. We'd poke our lips, blaming it for our having to eat Father's victuals. Oft Zard would crawl under the bed to sniffle, and Mother had to coax him out with morsels from her plate. He was two years old, and jealous of the baby. Fern never complained. She fetched milk and crusts to her hidden playhouse, eating little at the table. So it was Lark and I who stubbed at meals. A pone Father baked was a jander of soda. Vegetables were underdone or burnt. We would quarrel, saying spiteful things of the baby, though above our voices rose the screams of the locusts, "*Phar-rrr-a-oh! Pha-rrr-a-oh!*" The air was sick with their crying.

Father would blink at Mother. He'd hold his jaws, trying to keep a straight face. "No sense raising a babby nobody wants," he'd speak. "Wish I could swap her to a new set o' varmint traps. Or could I find a gypsy, I'd plumb give her away."

"I'd ruther to have a colt than a basketful o' baby chaps," I'd say. "I allus did want me one." I would think of our mare, and the promise Father once made. Long past he'd made it, longer than hope could live. He'd said, "Some fine pretty day thar might be a foal. Hit's on the books." But never would he say just when, never say it was a sure fact.

I recollect that on the morning the medicine drummer and his woman came down Shoal Creek I had gone into the bottom to hunt Fern's playhouse.

She had bragged of it, nettling me with her talk. "A witch couldn't unkiver my den," she'd said. "I got something there that'd skin yore eyes."

I was searching the berry thicket when a dingle-dangle sounded afar. A spring wagon rattled the stony creek-bed, pulled by a nag so small I could hardly believe it, and a man and woman rode the jolt seat. It passed the mill, climbing the steep road to our house. I watched it go, and hurried after; I ran, hoping it came unbeknownst to Fern.

But Fern was there before me, staring. Mother came onto the porch, taking her first steps in weeks. She held the baby, squinting in the light, her face pale as candlewax. Zard peeped around her skirts.

The drummer jumped to the ground, his hat crimped in a hand. He was oldy, and round-jawed as a cushaw is round, and not a hair grew on the pan of his head; he was old and his woman seemed young enough to be a daughter. He bowed to Mother, brushing his hat against the dirt. He spoke above the thresh of locusts, eying as if taking a size and measure. "Lady," he said, "could we bide a couple o' nights in your millhouse, we'd be grateful. My pony needs rest." The woman gazed. Her hair hung in plaits. She watched the baby in its bundle of clothes.

Mother sat down on the water bench. She couldn't stay afoot longer. "You're welcome to use," she replied. "A pity hit's full o' webs and meal dust. My man's off plowing, else he'd clean the brash out."

I couldn't hold my eyes off the nag, off the tossy mane that was curried and combed. She looked almost as pretty as a colt.

Fern edged nearer, anxious. "Lizards in that mill have got razor throats. You're liable to get cut at."

"We can pay," the drummer said to Mother.

"Not a pency-piece we'd take," Mother assured.

Fern became angry, and I marveled at her. She doubled fists behind her back. "Spiders beyond count in the mill. Spiders a-carrying nit bags and stingers."

"Lady," the drummer said, speaking to Mother and paying Fern no attention, "I've traveled a far piece in my life." He stacked his hands cakewise. "A host of sicknesses I've seen. Now, when a body needs a tonic, when their nerves stretch, I can tell on sight. I've seen women's flesh fall away like a snow melt. I've seen——"

"Doc Trawler!"

The woman had called from the wagon, calling a bit shrill and quick, tossing her plaits uneasily. She had seen Mother's face grow whiter than puccoon blossoms.

"Ask about the berries."

"Ah, yes," the drummer said irritably, dropping his hands. "My wife's a fool for berry cobbler. She's bound to eat though one seed can cause side-complaint. My special purge has saved her being stricken long ago."

"Ask may we pick berries in the bottom!" The woman's words cracked like broken sticks.

The drummer waited.

Mother stirred uncertainly. "Wild fruit's pizen as strickynine when locusts swarm," she cautioned. "Allus I've heard that."

The drummer's face lit, grinning. He swept his hat onto his head and climbed on the wagon. The woman smiled too, but it was the baby she smiled at.

"That mill's a puore varmint den," Fern spoke hatefully.

The pony wheeled, and they set off for the mill. The drummer's woman looked back, her eyes hard upon the baby.

That night we children sat at the table with empty plates. Grease frizzled the dove Father was cooking for Mother. "They hain't a finickier set o' chaps in Kentucky," Father groaned. "I bile stuff by the pot, I bake and I fry, still these young 'uns will hardly eat a mouthful. By jukes, if I don't believe they could live on blue air."

I wrinkled my nose. A musky smell came from somewhere. I spied at the bowl of potatoes, at the bud eyes staring. "I hain't hungry," I said, but I was. Hunger stalked inside of me.

The musk grew. Lark and Zard pinched their noses and grunted. Yet Fern didn't seem to mind. She spread her hands flat upon her plate, and they were pieded with candle-drip warts.

I grew envious of the warts. I bragged, "I've got a spool will blow soap bubbles the size o' yore head."

"Baby's got the world beat for bubbles," Father said. "Blows 'em with her mouth."

"A varmint's nigh," Mother said, covering the baby's face. She rocked her chair by the stove to fan the smell. "Traps ought to be set under the house."

Father poked a fork into the dove. "I met a skunk in the barnloft," he chuckled. "Stirred the shucks and out she come, tail high. I reckon it's my pea jacket by the door riching the wind."

"Polecats have got the prettiest tails of any critter," Fern defended. "Hain't allus a-miaowing like nannies."

"Their tails are not bonny as the drummer-pony's mane," I said.

"Haste that garment to the woodpile," Mother told me.

I snatched the jacket and went into the yard, leaving it on the chopblock. I looked about. The mulberry tree stood black-ripe with dark. Below, in the bottom, the mill cracks shone. I planned, "Come morning, I'll get a close view o' that nag. I'll say to the drummer, 'Was Poppy of a notion, would you swap to our mare?' " I spat, thinking of our beast.

Father was talking when I got back. "I've set traps the place o'er, but every day they're sprung, bait gone, and nothing snared. I say hit's a question. The only thing I've caught's an old she in the millhouse, and I figure little ones were weaned."

"Once I seed two varmints walking," Lark said. "I run, I did."

Fern stuck her chin out, vengeful and knowing. "I told them folks that mill was a puore den."

Mother saddened. "I've never heard a child talk so brashy to olders. I was ashamed."

Fern raised her hands, tick-tacking fingers. "Humph," she said willfully.

The thought came into my head that Fern's playhouse might be close to the mill. I stung to go and see.

"One thing's gospel," Father laughed, not wanting Mother to begin worrying, "chaps nor varmints won't tetch my bait. I load the traps and table, for nothing. They're independent as hogs on ice."

"These chaps are slipping out o' hand," Mother said, her lips trembling. "Fern, in partic'lar. Eleven years old and not a sign o' womanly pride. I can't recollect the last time she combed her hair."

"Might's well buy her breeches and call her a boy," Father teased, "yet I'm a-mind she'll break over. Girls allus get prissy by the time they're twelve. Hit's on the books." He eyed Lark and me. "I know two titmice hain't combed their topknots lately."

"You ought to make Fern wear plaits," I spoke. "The drummer's woman wears 'em."

"I hain't going to weave myself to ropes," Fern said. She walked fingers around her plate, skippety-hop. "Hair tails hanging. Humph! Ruther to be baldy."

"Ah, ho," Father laughed. "I come by the mill before dark and talked to Doc Trawler. I saw him with his hat off. Now, his woman don't need a looking-glass. She kin just say, 'Drap yore head down, old man. I aim to comb my lockets.' "

"Once I seed a horse go by with a wove tail," Lark said.

The dove browned, and was lifted to a plate. Father handed it to Mother. The bird was small, hard-fried, and briny it was bound to taste. Father always seasoned with a heavy hand. I thought, "It would take a covey o' doves to satisfy me." I felt that empty. I thought of berries wasting in the bottom; I thought of the mulberry tree. I spooned a half-cooked potato from the bowl, speaking under my breath, "That baby's to blame. She hain't nothing but a locust-bug."

Mother fiddled with the bird. Zard slid off the bench to get a morsel. Presently Mother gave it all to him, saying, "I can't stir an appetite. I can't force it down."

Father groaned. "Be-dabs, if the whole gin-works hain't got the punies. Even the mare tuck a spell today. She wouldn't eat corn nor shuck."

"What ails the mare?" Mother asked quietly, The baby had whimpered in her nap.

I didn't pity the beast, being contemptuous of her. I scoffed, "Bet they's folks would say hit's writ in a book. Now, they's no book got everything printed already."

Father answered neither Mother nor me, but his eyes were sharp and bright. He said, "I forgot that drummer sent a bottle o' tonic. Swore it'd red the blood and quick the appetite. Hit's yonder in my pea jacket. One o' you fellers fotch it."

"I be to go," Lark said. He brought in a tall bottle of yellow medicine.

Father held the bottle aloft, jesting, "If this would arouse hunger, I'd dose chaps, traps, and the mare. Allus been said, when the sick take to eating, they're nigh well. A shore promise." He set the bottle on a high shelf and chuckled. "I wonder from what creek Doc Trawler dipped that yaller water."

"Is the mare's sickness natural?" Mother insisted.

"I heard a gander honk last fall," Father said, "but hit's no sign we've got a goose nest."

Lark said, "I bet she up and et berries."

"Old plug mare," I mumbled. I spoke aloud, "That drummer's got a healthy nag. Hain't much bigger'n a colt. Was she mine, I'd not swap for gold."

"I glimpsed that play-pretty of a nag," Father said. "She's old as Methuselum's grandpappy's uncle. Teeth wore to the gum. Thar she was eating out o' a plate, like two-legged folks. If a woman hain't got chaps to spile, she'll pamper a critter to death. The way with women."

The baby waked suddenly, crying. Father leaned over Mother's shoulder. He clucked. "See her ope her eyes?"

I said, "Ruther to hear a bullfrog croaker."

Lark scowled. "Wust I come on a little 'un nested in a stump, I'd run far and not go back."

Fern twickled her warty fingers at me and Lark; she made a hop-frog of her hands. She knew how to rile us.

"Woe, woe," Father moaned. "I reckon we might's well give this child to the drummer-woman and be done. She's got nothing to pet on but that nag and bald-head man."

I looked squarely at Fern. "I've a fair notion where your play-house is," I said. "I'm going a-searching."

"Humph," Fern said, but she became uneasy. She rubbed her hands together, flaking the tallow warts. "Unkiver my play-nest and I'll get level with you. I'll pay back double."

Mother sighed, "If a pot o' soup could be made tomorrow, I believe I could eat. Soup with a light seasoning." She rocked her chair impatiently as Fern and I kept quarreling. "I long to tame these chaps," she said.

"You'd have to do what Old Daniel Tucker done in his song," Father said. "Comb their heads with a wagon wheel."

The mulberries were ripe. They hung like caterpillars, ready to fall at a touch. I sat high in the tree crotch among zizzing locusts, longing to taste the berries, and watching Fern. I saw

Fern crawl under the house; I saw her skitter up the barn-loft ladder. She went here and yon, and was gone, and never could a body tell where.

I hurried toward the mill. The cow tunnels winding through high growth in the bottom were empty. I listened. A beetle-bug snapped and a bird made clinky sounds. I heard digging. A thing went *rutch rutch* in dirt. I tipped-toed; I craned my neck. There amid tall briers the drummer knelt, digging herb roots. The pan or his head was glassy in the sun.

"Did some'un go this way?" I asked.

The drummer rested. Sweat drops beaded his forehead. "While ago a skunk come in smelling distance. I had to stopple my nose." He sorted the roots, pressing them between his thumbs until sap oozed; he frowned and the meat of his jaws tautened. "It's the contrary season to gather herbs, yit a kettle o' tonic's got to be brewed ere I set off tomorry." He plucked a weed sprig from his grab pocket. "Only coma I find more o' this ratsbane."

"I know where they's a passel," I said.

His face slackened. "Help me gather some and I'll be obliged. I can pay."

I cut my eyes about, ashamed to say the thing I'd planned. The words pricked my tongue. I took note that blackberries grew large as a toe in the bottom, and both hunger and the pony grew in my mind. "Would you be in a notion swapping your nag to our mare?" I ventured at last. "I allus did want me a little beast."

"Fifteen years we've fed that pony," the drummer said. He arose, stretching his legs. "She's nigh a family member, and my wife thinks more o' that nag than she does her victuals. She'd skulp me, was I to trade."

How bitter I felt toward our mare. "Our critter'll never have a colt like it was promised," I grumbled.

The drummer stacked his hands. He looked wise as a county judge. "She needs a special medicine," he advised. "I mix a tonic that cures any ill, fixes up and straightens out man or beast— the biggest medicine ever wrapped in glass." He patty-caked his palms. "Now, there's one trade I do fancy. Show me where the ratsbane grows and I'll make you a present of a bottle. One's all I've got left."

I spoke, "Bet was a feller to eat wild fruit, a dram o' that tonic would cuore the pizen. I bet."

A woman's voice called from the mill. "Doc Trawler! Oh, Doc!"

The drummer started off. "You stay till I see what my wife's after," he said. I waited, and soon heard him returning, and the cow tunnels were filled with his laughter. He came back shaking with merriment. "That devil of a pony!" he said. "Oh, hit's a good thing we're leaving tomorry."

We went to grabble ratsbane and the drummer chuckled all day. He was a fool about that nag. We dug till my back sprung; we dug till the sun-ball stooped in the sky.

Late in the afternoon we stood by the mill with a poke crammed full of roots. I breathed in the smell of cooking victuals and fairly starved. The drummer slapped the poke; he treated it like a human being. "I'll get your pay," he said, and fetched a bottle out of the mill, a bottle no taller than my uncle-finger. "Hit's strong as Samson," he said. "And wait. My wife's fixing something for your mother."

"Is this medicine bound to work?" I asked, sliding the bottle inside of a pocket.

"Hit'll fix that mare right up, shore as Sunday-come-Monday."

The nag walked around the millhouse. She stuck her head in at the door, and drew back crunching an apple. The drummer smiled. "See that thar. Didn't I say this hardtail's nigh one o' the family?"

"My colt's going to have folk sense," I bragged.

"This pony's bound to stick her noggin into places," the drummer said. His face wrinkled happily. The crown or his head shone. "Now, what do you reckon she found this morning? A chap's playhouse. Leave it to a long-nose beast to sniff things out. Me and my wife looked, and what we saw we couldn't believe, but thar it was to prove."

"I'd give a pretty to know," I pleaded. "I've got to larn."

The drummer frowned. "For a good reason I don't want that place disturbed till we leave." He scratched his headtop, undecided whether to tell. "Swear you won't take a look till we're on the road and gone?"

" 'Pon my word and deed."

"Hit's yonder then," he said, pointing to the lower side of the millhouse where the floor rested on high pillars. "I can't blame your sister for trying to scare us with talk o' spiders and lizards. Oh, she's a wild 'un."

The drummer's woman brought a bowl capped with a lid. The plaits of her hair tipped her shoulders, and her eyes were sad as a ewe's. "Reckon we could steal a child off these folks?" she joked her man. "Five in their house. One wouldn't be missed." She handed the bowl to me. "Take this cobbler to your mother. Tell her every berry's been split; tell it's safe to eat."

I ran home, and my heart pounded as I went.

Mother sat alone with the baby. Father stirred soup in the kitchen, and I heard Lark and Zard quarreling there. I uncovered the cobbler, reaching it to Mother. The sweety smell rose in my face. My mouth watered. I spoke loudly, for Mother had plugs of wool in her ears to dim the cry of locusts; I said what the drummer's woman told me to say. The baby leaned to see. Then we heard Father coming, and Lark and Zard following. Mother whispered quickly, "I'm grateful, and hit's a pity to waste, yet we can't trust eating berries. Haste the cobble-pie to the pig pen, and don't name to the others." But time was only left to shove the bowl under the bed.

"All the locusts in Egypt couldn't make a racket equaling these two," Father told Mother. "Fussing o'er nothing but who could blow the largest spool bubble. I mixed hope with that soup you'd soon be up and at these young 'uns. I biled enough to last two days."

"I'll mend once the plague's ended," Mother said. "Any day now the locusts will hush. I long to give these chaps a taste o' soap and water."

"Fern come into the kitchen," Father said, "and it tuck a minute to tell be she varmint or vixen. Hit'd worry the mare's currycomb to thrash the burrs."

Zard peeked at the baby and sulled. He was green jealous. He dropped to his knees and crawled toward the bed. He scampered under.

"Another sight I glimpsed today," Father went on, "and hit was that drummer's woman combing a nag's mane. I never stayed to see if she bowed it with ribbons." He turned upon me, keeping his face sober. "And I've looked up our mare in the books. One more page-leaf to turn before knowing when."

"Only would Fern take a lesson," Mother said uneasily, making a sign. I snatched the bowl, and neither Lark nor Father noticed, for Mother raised the baby's head. Father chuckled, "See the bubble she's pucked with her mouth. Beats any you fellers can blow."

"No bigger'n a pea," Lark discounted.

Father snapped a thumb and forefinger. "Be-jibs, if we hain't got to get rid o' this little 'un. Not a kind word's allowed her."

I stole away to the pig pen, uncovered the bowl, and found the berry cobbler half eaten. Zard had gobbled it. I was fearful, believing him poisoned, thinking he might die. I remembered the bottle of medicine. Could I persuade him to swallow a dose? A thought sprung in my head. I'd dose all—the mare, Mother, and Zard. The drummer had vowed it would straighten out man or beast. They'd take medicine, and not know.

I hastened to the barn, pouring a knuckle's depth of the medicine into a scoop of oats. The mare poked her great yellow tongue into the grain; she ground her teeth. She ate the last bit, and licked the trough. She was mighty fat, I recollect.

On I hied to the house. I tipped inside the kitchen. There was the soup pot boiling on the stove, and I emptied nearly all of the medicine into it. All but one draft went into the soup.

Suddenly a *tick tick* sounded behind the stove. I thrust the bottle pocket-deep, and looked. It was Fern, hidden with a comb in her hand.

"Humph," Fern said, hiding the comb. I could scarcely see her eyes through a brush of hair. She spoke threateningly, "I saw that baldy drummer show you where my playhouse is. If you go there, they's something will scare yore gizzard."

"Humph," I said, mocking.

The next morning the locusts had hushed. Cast skins clung to trunks and boughs, and it was as quiet as the first day of the world. Ere dew dried I waited in the bottom for the drummer folk to go. So great the stillness was, my breath seemed a thunder in my chest. I saw the drummer and his woman climb into their wagon and drive up-hill to our house; I saw Father shake the drummer's hand in farewell. Fern, Lark, and Zard were staring.

I crept to the lower side of the mill where the floor stood high. I crawdabbed under. Nothing I saw in Fern's playhouse, nothing save four stone pillars growing up, and an empty pan sitting. "Humph," I thought.

I heard footsteps. I sprang behind a pillar. Fern came underneath the floor bringing a cup of milk and meat crumbs; she brought the bait from Father's traps. Her hair was combed slick and two plaits tipped her shoulders, woven like the drummer-woman's. My mouth fell open.

The milk was poured into the pan. Fern squatted beside it, calling, "Biddy, biddy, biddy," and four little polecats came walking to lap the milk, and three big varmints began to nibble the meat. I blinked, shivering with fright, and of a sudden the critters knew I was there, and Fern knew. The polecats vanished like weasel smoke.

I recollect Fern's anger. She didn't cry. She sat pale as any blossom, narrowing her eyes at me. But not a mad or meany word she spoke. The thing she said came measured and cold between tight lips.

"You hain't heard the baby's been tuck," she said. "Poppy give it to the drummer."

I stood frozen, more frightened than any varmint scare. When I could move I ran toward the house, running with loss aching inside of me.

I thrust my head in at the door. Father was carving spool pipes for Lark and Zard, Mother ate soup out of a bowl, and her lap and arms were empty. Mother was saying, "Now this is the best soup ever I did eat. Hit's seasoned just right."

Father grinned. "You can allus tell when a body's getting well. They'll eat a feller out o' house and home." He saw me standing breathlessly in the door; he laughed, not trying to keep his face grave. "Well, well," he said, "I've closed the books on that mare. A colt's due tomorrow or the next day. That's a shore fact."

"The baby!" I choked. "She's been tuck!"

"Baby?" Father asked, puzzled. "Why, thar she kicks on the bed, a-blowing bubbles and growing bigger'n the government."

I turned, running away in shame and joy. I ran out to the mulberry tree. The fruit had fallen and the ground was like a great pie. I drew the medicine bottle from my pocket; I swallowed the last dose. I ate a bellyful of mulberries.

The Stir-Off

"COME FRIDAY FOR the sorghum making," Jimp Buckheart sent word to me by Father. "Come to the stir-off party, and take a night."

Father chuckled as he told, knowing I had never stayed away from home. Father said, "Hit's time you larnt other folks' ways. Now, Old Gid Buckheart's family lives fat as horse traders. He's got five boys, tough as whang leather, though nary a one's a match to Gid himself; and he's the pappy o' four girls who're picture-pieces." He teased as he whittled a molassy spoon for me. "Mind you're not captured by one o' Gid's daughters. They're all pretty, short or tall, every rung o' the ladder." He teased enough to rag his tongue. I grunted scornfully, but I was tickled to go. I'd heard Jimp had a flying-jinny, and kept a ferret.

Jimp met me before noon at their land boundary. Since last I'd seen him he had grown; and he jerked his knees walking and cocked his head birdwise, imping his father. He was Old Gid Buckheart over again. He didn't stand stranger. "Kin you keep secrets?" he asked. "Hold things and not let out?" I nodded. Jimp said, "My pap's going to die death hearing Plumey's marrying Rant Branders tonight at the stir-off. Pap'll never give up to her picking such a weaky looking feller." His face brightened with pride. "I'm the only one knows. Rant aims to hammer me a pair o' brass knuckles if I play hush-mouth, a pair my size. He swore to it."

"Hit's not honest to fight with knucks unless a feller's bigger'n you," I said.

"I'm laying for my brother Bailus," Jimp explained. "He's older'n me, and allus tricking, and trying to borrow or steal my ferret. I'd give my beastie to git him ducked in the sorghum hole."

"I long to see your ferret," I said. "I'm bound to ride the fly-jinny."

"Bailus wants to sick my ferret into rabbit nests," Jimp complained. "Hit's a ferret's nature to skin alive. Ere I'd let Bailus borrow, I'd crack its neck. Ruther to see it dead."

We walked a spell. Roosters crowed midday. We topped a knob and afar in a hollow stood the Buckhearts' great log house, and beyond under gilly trees was the sorghum gin.

Jimp pointed. "Peep Eye's minding hornets off the juice barrel, and I reckon everybody else's eating. We've made two runs o' sirup already, dipped enough green skims to nigh fill the sorghum hole, and cane's milled for the last."

Hounds raced to meet us. We halted a moment by the beegums. On bowed heads of sunflowers redbirds were cracking seeds. Jimp gazed curiously at me, cocking his chin. "You and me's never fit," he said. "Fellers don't make good buddies till they prove which can out-do."

We waded the hounds to the kitchen, spying through the door. Jimp's father and brothers were eating and his mother and three of his sisters passed serving dishes; and in the company chair sat Squire Letcher, making balls of his bread, and cutting eyes at the girls. Jimp told me their names. The squire I knew already; I knew he was the Law, and a widow-man. "Hardhead at the end o' the bench is Bailus," Jimp said. "Plumey's standing behind Pap—the one's got a beauty spot." Plumey was fairest of the three girls, fair as a queeny blossom. Her cheek bore a mole speck, like a spider with tucked legs; and a born mole it was, not one stuck on for pretty's sake. Jimp told me all of the names, then said, "I wonder what that law-square's a-doing here?"

We clumped inside. Old Gid spoke a loud howdy-do, asking after my folks, and Mrs. Buckheart tipped the cowlick on my head. A chair was drawn for me, and victuals brought to heap my plate. Bailus leaned to block Jimp's way to his seat on the bench, so Jimp had to crawl under the table. He stuck his head up, mad-faced, gritting his teeth. "Ho, Big Ears," Bailus said. The older brothers sat with eyes cold upon Squire Letcher. The squire was a magistrate and bound to put a damper on the stir-off party.

Gid pushed back his chair and spiked his elbows, watching the foxy glances of Squire Letcher. "We're old-timey people," he told the squire, his words querulous. "We may live rough, but we're lacking nothing. For them with muscle and backbone, Troublesome Creek country is the land o' plenty." He swept an arm toward gourds of lard, strings of lazy wife beans, and shelves of preserves; he snapped his fingers at cushaws hanging by vine tails. "We raise our own living, and once the house and barns are full we make friends with the earth. We swear not to hit it another lick till spring."

Squire Letcher popped three bread balls into his mouth, swallowed, and was done with his meal. He crossed his knife and fork in a mannerly fashion. "Don't skip the main harvest," he sighed in his fullness. "Nine in this family, and none married yet." He smirked, looking sideways at the girls. "But you can't hide blushy daughters in the head of a hollow for long. Single men will be wearing your doorsteps down."

Gid's voice lifted peevishly. "A beanstalk of a feller has made tracks here already, a shikepoke I've never met, a stranger tee-total."

Plumey's cheeks burnt. The mole on her cheek seemed to inch a grain.

Gid went on, "Why a girl o' mine would choose a man so puny is beyond reckoning. I'd vow he's not got the strength to raise a proper living."

Mrs. Buckheart spoke up, taking Plumey's part. "An old hornbeam's muscles show through the bark, but ne'er a growing oak's. And I say you'll ne'er meet a feller with your head allus turned."

The squire flushed merrily. "Gideon, thar's few longing to shake your hand. You'd put a man to his knees or break bones. Recollect I've yet to clap your paw? Oh, you're the fistiest old man running free."

The shag of Gid's brows raised, uncovering eyes blue as millpond water. "One thing I do recollect," Gid said, "a thing going years past when we were young scrappers." He cocked his head. "I recall we battled like rams once. We wore the ground out, tuggety-pull. But it was a draw."

The squire caught the Buckheart boys' hard gaze. He sobered, shifting uneasily, ready to leave the table. Law papers rustled in his pockets. "Gid," he insisted, rising, "you're of an older set. We never ran together, never wrestled as I remember. I'd swear before a Grand Jury."

"I hain't so old I whistle when I talk," Gid crowed. "Hain't so old but what I'd crack skulls with anybody. Jist any sweet time I kin grab a churn dasher and make butter o' airy one o' my sons." A grin twisted his mouth as he got up. "Now, Square, we shore fit. We did." And Squire Letcher and Gid went off arguing into the midst of the house.

"Who invited that walking courthouse?" Cirius blurted.

"Old jury hawk," U Z said.

"He might have come for a good purpose," Mrs. Buckheart chided. "Eat your victuals."

Before we left the table Gid came back. "I've voted the square into going bird-hunting," he said. "Atter his dinner settles one o' you boys hustle him o'er the hills and bring him back so dogtired he'll start home afore dark."

"I'll go," Bailus volunteered, puffing his jaws, mocking the squire. "I'll wade thorns and walk cliff faces. I'll wear his soles off."

"Travel the starch out o' him," Gid said. "I've a notion he oughten to stay on."

"Who asked that magistrate here anyhow?" John asked, his face sour as whey. "They's more warrants in his pockets than a buzzard's got feathers."

Leander said, "He'll plague the stir-off. Fellers will think he's come a-summonsing. And I've heard a mighty crowd's coming across the ridge tonight."

"We've only invited neighbors and a couple o' fiddlers," Gid spoke fractiously, "but a rambling widower is apt to come unbid any place. Yet I'm more concerned about a tender sprig of a feller who's shore to be here, one I'd ruther see going than com-ing, ruther to see the span o' his back than his face."

Plumey paled whiter than a hen-and-biddy dish. The boys grunted.

Old Gid began to lay down the law. "Girls!" he said, "you're not to throw necks tonight staring at the boys. Sons! We're going to mark the sorghum hole. We're making puore molasses, and no candy jacks. Keep a watch on the kettle."

"I choose pull-candy to sirup," Jimp said.

I thought in my head, "I bet candy jacks would be good."

U Z groaned, "Pap's bounden to dry up the party."

Old Gid's face softened. He chuckled at me and Jimp gobbling pie. "You tadwhackers better save a big leetle spot for the molassy foam."

"Pappy," Jimp asked, "did you and the square sheep-fight once, a-butting heads?"

Old Gid raised his brows and grinned. He stepped to the door and called Peep Eye to dinner.

"I aim to see your ferret," I reminded Jimp. "I want to ride the fly-jinny."

We crept into the smokehouse where the ferret was kept hidden. "A feller can't take a step withouten Peep Eye's watching," Jimp complained, latching the door. In that darksome place I saw giant pumpkins squatting on hard earth, and fat squashes crooking yellow necks. I saw a bin of Amburgey apples, a mort of victuals in kegs and jars; I set eyes on three barrels of molasses. I said, "Them many sirups will turn strong as bull beef ere they can be et."

Jimp whistled a sketch. A furry head lifted above a sack of capping corn. I jumped in fright, and the varmint started, jerking its head down, burrowing into the sack. The ferret wouldn't come out then for all our begging and poking cobs. I didn't get to see the whole of him.

"He's scared," I said.

"My beastie's got nerve spite o' playing timid," Jimp defended. "He'll tackle critters double his size, jist like fisty people. Cagey ones don't show their nerve till they come to a pinch." And Jimp made a wry face, laughing suddenly. He popped his hands together. "I'd give my ferret to see Pap and the square lock horns."

"I'd ruther to see your father shake hands with Rant Branders," I said, knowing by looks that Squire Letcher was snailweak. "Rant might be tough as whang leather."

"My pap could make Rant eat straw."

"A man's backbone don't print through his clothes."

We listened a bit, our ears against the door; we stole outside, looking sharp. "Yonder's Bailus coming," Jimp whispered, and began to run. I ran after him, though it wasn't Bailus I'd seen. I had glimpsed a girl-child staring around a corner, and she was a Buckheart, for she bore their presence. She had jerked her head away quicker than any ferret.

We ran till the wind burnt out of us; we stopped to rest in a weed patch where noggin sticks grew tall and brittle. "I saw a girl yon side the smokehouse," I said when I could speak. "I bet she heard a plenty."

"Peep Eye," Jimp said. "You can't say 'gizzard' withouten her hearing."

"Reckon she's larnt about Plumey and Rant?"

"Now, no. Hit's the first time ever I did know a thing afore her." Jimp thought a moment. "Was it Peep Eye growed up and marrying off, I'd be tickled. Me, I hain't ne'er going to marry."

"I'm not aiming to be a widow-man," I said, anxious to go to the flying-jinny. I gathered a dozen noggin sticks, snapping them at the root. Their woody knots were like small fists. Jimp picked a bunch too, saying, "Let's crack each other's skulls and see who hollers first."

I winced, dreading the pain, but I wouldn't be out-done. "You hit first," I said.

"No, you."

"I hain't mad. I can't hit cold."

"I'll rile you," Jimp said. He furrowed his brows and spoke a lie-tale. "Yore pappy steals money off dead men's eyeballs, and yore folks feeds on carr'n crows."

I struck, breaking the weed. Jimp cracked one across my noggin. We broke five sticks apiece, and felt for goose eggs on our heads. Then we went on to the flying-jinny at the pasture gap, and there stood Bailus, waiting.

Bailus's face was grave. You could tell he had come begging. "Big Ears," he began, "you ought to lend a hand gitting rid o' the magistrate, else the stir-off will be a reg'lar funeral."

Jimp poked his lips. "Jist a trick to borrow my ferret. You got no use for him bird-hunting."

"The square wants to hole a rabbit or two."

"Hain't fair to skin varmints alive. I'm not loaning, and that's the God's truth."

I studied the flying-jinny, noting its pattern in my head. I felt bound to have Father make one. A long hickory pole it was, pegged in the middle to a sourwood stump. I straddled the limber end of the pole, hungry to ride.

Bailus's eyes narrowed. "I've heard a bee-swarm o' folks are coming tonight, a drove o' people we've not invited. They's something fotching 'em here. Now, loan yore ferret and I'll tell what." He sniffled, but I saw it was make-like. "Creek water hain't dull as a stir-off with a magistrate keeping tab."

Jimp scoffed. He turned toward me. "I'll give you the first ride."

"Fellers!" Bailus spoke quickly, "both o' you hop on and I'll push."

Though Jimp's face grew long with doubt he straddled the jinny. We latched our legs about the hickory pole. Bailus began to push, slowly at first, digging his toes into the ground. As the pole swung clear he pushed faster, faster, around and around. We sped. We traveled swifter than a live jinny. A wind caught in my shirt, jerking the tails. I hunkered against the log; I held on for bare life. The earth whirled, trees went walking, and tiptops of the mountains swayed and rail fences climbed straight into the sky. My hands numbed, and my chest seemed near to bursting. My fingers loosened, and I was tossed into the air.

I lay on the ground, stupid with dizziness, and Jimp wove drunkenly, trying to stand. Bailus was nowhere in sight. Then I saw three bright faces, three girl-chaps melting together. My lids went blinkety-blink-blink. When my head cleared I saw it was Peep Eye, alone. She was the spit image of Plumey, though she had no mole on her cheek; she was the prettiest human being ever I did see.

"Air you been dranking john corn?" Peep Eye teased.

"I been ding-donged enough," Jimp blurted. "I'd swap them knucks I'm promised to even up with Bailus."

"He's hasted to steal your ferret," Peep Eye said. "He'll have it and gone ere you kin catch him."

Jimp kicked the ground in anger. "I wish that critter was dead and dust. I do."

Peep Eye stood pretty as a bunty bird. Jimp and I leaned giddily against the jinny pole. Peep Eye said, "I know something you fellers don't. Plumey's marrying Rant Branders tonight."

"Be-doggies," Jimp swore. "Rant promised I was the only one to know. Secrets nor varmints nobody can keep."

"One secret I've kept," Peep Eye bragged. "I've larnt why the square's here. A scanty few knows that."

We pleaded with her to tell, but she wouldn't. She would only talk of the wedding. "When I grow as tall and fair as Plumey," she said, "I'm going to pick me a man who can jounce air one o' my brothers, one strong as Pappy, and able to take his part."

"By doomsday you won't be fair as Plumey," Jimp said contrarily.

Peep Eye frowned. Her month puckered.

"You're the born image of Plumey," I said, "except for a beauty spot. Now, I choose a mole on a woman's cheek."

"I kin make me one out o' a soot pill," Peep Eye said.

"Be-doggies," Jimp grumbled. "I hain't ever aiming to marry."

I sat on the pole and swung my legs. "I'll not be a bachelor or a widow-man," I spoke.

Peep Eye looked strangely at me. She raised her arms and pushed me backward, and fled. I stood on my head yon side the jinny.

Jimp said, "Girls allus let a feller know when they like him a mite."

UNDER THE SIRUP kettle fire blazed so lively the darkness was eaten away, and pale glimmers of lanterns swallowed, and far tops of the gilly trees lit. I sat on a heap of milled sorghum stalks, my molassy spoon ready, anxious to taste the foam. Jimp crouched beside me, grinding his teeth in anger. He'd heard his ferret was dead, and he stared auger holes at Bailus and Squire Letcher. Oh, Bailus hadn't got rid of the squire. The squire rested on an empty keg, sighing wearily and clapping a hand to his mouth.

I had Jimp point Rant Branders out. Rant appeared bare-bones, yet in height he stood taller than the Buckhearts. He was long armed and long legged, and a grain awkward. I said, "I bet he's a cagey one. He's a green grasshopper of a man." And I began counting the people who had come to the stir-off. I named my fingers five times and over. I saw Plumey whispering to a bunch of girls, and Old Gid moseying around wondering at the crowd, and Peep Eye flitting here and yon like a silk butterfly. I kept gazing at Peep Eye.

"My beastie's stone dead," Jimp glummed. "That law-square and Bailus's to blame. Had I a chip o' money I'd hire fellers to trick them into the sorghum hole. Be-dogs, I would."

"Fellers'd be scared of a magistrate," I said. "Anyhow, your ferret wasn't shot a-purpose. Hit was mistook for a rabbit."

"My pap hain't afeared o' the Law. He could scare that square in without tipping him."

I caught Peep Eye watching me, and I wanted to leave the sorghum heap. I saw her face was pouty and cold. I thought inside my head, "Hit's not like what Jimp said. I bet she hates my gizzard," but I said aloud to Jimp, "I'm bound to eat molassy foam when it's first done. Hain't but one thing better, and that's pull-candy."

Jimp harped his troubles. "Rant's broke his swear-word. He promised me knucks to fit, and then made 'um shooting big. They'd fit U Z." He fetched them from a pocket and the finger places were the size of quarter-dollars. "I've struck an idee I don't want that fence rail for a brother-in-law. Oh, my pap could jounce him with one arm tied."

"Rant hain't grown yit," I said. "He might grow thick. Already he's a high tall feller."

We went to stand by the sirup kettle, breathing the mellow steam hungrily, watching the golden foam rise. Leander chunked the fire and U Z ladled green skimmings into the sorghum hole. The hole was waist-deep and marked by a butterweed stalk. U Z joked us, "Dive in, boys, and you kin stand yore breeches in a corner tonight." We stepped warily.

Old Gid came with Mrs. Buckheart to test the sirup, spinning drops off of chips, tasting. Gid said, "Stir till it 'gins making sheep's eyes, and mind not to over-bile." He stared unbelievingly at the crowd. "Only a funeral occasion or a marrying would draw such a swarm, and I've heard o' nobody dying. Yet, for a host o' folks, they're terrible quiet."

"Bury some'un in the sorghum hole," U Z laughed, "and they'll liven up."

"I long to see the Law eat a few skims," Leander said, and Peep Eye was hiding behind him, hearing every word.

U Z said, "I'm for giving the oninvited something to recollect this stir-off by."

"Amen," Leander said.

Mrs. Buckheart spoke nervously. "We ought to o' saved a couple gallons o' juice for candy, to please the chaps. We've got more sirup now than can be sopped till Jedgment."

"Invited or not," Gid said, "I want folks to pleasure themselves. What's become o' the fiddlers?"

Leander shrugged. "Ever hear of a fiddler loving the Law? They high-tailed."

Old Gid cocked his chin and spoke low. "The size o' this crowd is onnatural. Something's drawed folks."

Jimp's mouth opened, but he'd no chance to get a word in edgeways. Gid latched his thumbs on his galluses and spiked his elbows. "I'm not a born fool," he said, "Why, I know the magistrate come to speak a ceremony. Everybody knows. Even Peep Eye's got the fact writ on her face." He glanced defiantly at Mrs. Buckheart. "Woman! That spindling Branders stranger couldn't make a hum-bird a living."

Mrs. Buckheart's neck reddened. "Stranger to nobody but you. You've ne'er tested his grit, to my knowing."

"Why a daughter o' mine would choose a shikepoke to live with is ontelling."

Peep Eye emerged from behind Leander, "Plumey worships the dirt betwixt Rant Branders's toes," she said. She threw her neck like a hen; she flicked a spiteful glance at me.

My hunger fled. I thought, "I'll not eat a bite o' Buckheart foam," and I tossed the molassy spoon into the fire. I turned away and saw Jimp whispering to U Z; I saw Jimp thrust the brass knuckles into U Z's hand.

Old Gid snapped, "Tell that young jake to git his growth."

"Speak to his face," Mrs. Buckheart challenged. "Come, I'll acquaint you."

"Sick him, Pap," Jimp crowed happily.

Gid's brows raised. "Ah," he said. His woman had him cornered. "Ah," he mumbled, "I don't mind shaking Rant Branders's glass hand, but first let me blow a spark o' life into the gethering." And just then Jimp raised on tiptoe, calling, "Looky yonder.

They's two fellers rooster-fighting." Two fellows had their feet on marks, their arms doubled. They smote each other.

"Be-dog," Jimp cried, "wisht I was rooster-fighting with some'un my size." We hustled to see, crawling between folks' legs, getting inside of the circle.

The rooster-fighters halted and the gathering made a roar of joy for Old Gid stepped into the ring, walked past Rant, and leveled a finger at Squire Letcher. Gid's voice rose goodnaturedly. "Me and the square have a bone to pick. Allus ago we fit, and nary a one could whoop."

A flat smile withered on the squire's cheeks. He'd not the chance of a rabbit scrapping a ferret.

Gid said, "Let's move nigher the fire for light."

The crowd moved, leading the squire; it pushed and spread until the sorghum hole lay inside the ring. The butterweed stalk vanished. I saw Old Gid's boys bunching behind the crowd, their faces bright and tricky. U Z had left the kettle, edging close to Bailus; and both Leander and Bailus grinned oddly at me and Jimp.

But Gid didn't tip the squire. The magistrate stepped off the marked line, giving up ere he'd begun. He didn't even box his arms. He walked backward, keeping Gid at arm's length; he sidled and crawdabbed until he had sorghum-holed himself. He came out green as a mossed turkle. And then it was Old Gid's boys began pushing, and fellows shoved and fought to keep clear of the hole. Jimp and I were in the midst of the battle. Gid's boys soused a plenty; they soused folk invited or not, and they ducked one another too. U Z grabbed Bailus, rolling him in headforemost; and Leander caught me, and Bailus snagged Jimp. They dipped us.

I wiped the green skims off my face. I saw Old Gid walk up to Rant Branders, saying, "Hit's time we're acquainted," and stuck out his arm. They clapped hands. Gid's jaws clenched as he gripped, his neck corded. Yet Rant didn't give down, didn't bat an eye, or bend a knee. He stood prime up to Old Gid, and wouldn't be conquered.

Old Gid dropped his hand. He cut a glance about, chuckling. "Roust the square if they's to be a wedding," he said. "Night's a-burning."

Jimp and I hid behind the cane pile, being too hang-headed and shy to watch a marrying. Under the gilly trees Jimp said, "Me and you hain't never fit. Fighting makes good buddies." He clenched his fists.

I knew Peep Eye spied upon us. "You hit first," I said, acting cagey, taking my part.

"Say a thing to rile me."

I said, "Yore pappy's a bully man, and I'm glad Rant Branders locked his horns."

We fought. We fought with bare fists, and it was tuggety-pull, and neither of us could out-do. And of a sudden Peep Eye stood between us. Her cheek bore a soot mole, and she was fairer than any finch of a bird, fairer even than Plumey. She raised a hand, striking me across the mouth, and ran. Jimp said, "Jist a love lick." The blow hurt, but I was proud.

And then we heard Old Gid's voice ring like a bell, and saw him waving his arms by the forgotten molasses kettle. "Land o' Gravy!" he shouted. "We've made seventeen gallons o' candy jacks."

On Quicksand Creek

Aaron Splicer drove a bunch of yearlings into our yard on a March evening. Heifers bawled and young bullies made raw cries. We hurried out into the cold dark of the porch. Aaron rode up to the doorsteps, and Father called to him, not knowing at first who he was. "Hello?" Father spoke, and when he knew it was Aaron, called heartily, " 'Light and shake the weather."

Aaron opened his fleeced collar, rustling new leather. His breath curled a fog. "If this Shoal Creek mud gets any deeper," he called, "it'll be beyond traveling. A horse bogs to the knees." He slid to the ground, limbering his legs.

Father led Aaron's horse into the mare's stall. He brought a brass-trimmed saddle onto the porch. Aaron shook his boots, loosening mud balls, letting them fall on the steps. His tracks smudged the floors. Mother prepared a meal for him, our supper having long been eaten; and Lark and Zard and Fern pried at Aaron with their eyes. I studied his leather clothes: ox-yellow coat, belt wide as a grist mill's, fancy boots. I'd never seen boots matching the ones he wore. Father had a costly pair, a pair worth eighteen dollars, yet they weren't lengthy, or pin-pointed, or hid-stitched like Aaron Splicer's.

Aaron shucked off his coat. A foam of sheep's wool lined the underside. "Thar's not a cent in yearlings," he said. "Hit's jist swapping copper for brass. Beef steers are what puts sugar in the gourd, and nary a one I've found betwixt here and the head of Left Hand Fork."

"Crate Thompson cleaned the steers out o' all the creeks forking Troublesome," Father said. "I've heard a sketch about him being on Quicksand now. I reckon they's a sight o' beef in the neighborhood o' Decoy and Handshoe."

Mother brought a plate of creaseback beans, buttered cushaw, and a sour-sweet nubbin of pickled corn. Fern raked coals upon the hearth for the coffeepot. While Aaron ate, Father had me and Lark brighten Aaron's boots. We scraped the caked mud away, rubbed on tallow, and spat on the leather. We polished them with linsey rags until they shone.

"I never saw boots have such sharpening toes," Father said. "You could nigh pick a splinter out o' yore finger with them." He thrust his own boots forth to show the bluntness of the shoecaps. "But cattlemen allus crave leather with trimmings."

Our cats leapt upon my knees. They watched Aaron, twitching their whiskers, tensing their spines; they held crafty oblong eyes upon him. I thought, "I'm liable to be a cattleman when I'm grown up, and go traveling far. Yet it'd take a spell to get used to thorny boots. I'd be ashamed to wear 'em."

Aaron finished eating, wiped his chin with the hairy back of a hand, and walked his chair nearer the fire. Father offered him a twist of home-raised tobacco. He bit a chew, stretching the poles of his legs to the hearth, saying, I'd take a short cut to Quicksand if I didn't have these yearlings on my neck. Maybe I'd get thar before Crate Thompson buys every last steer." He rubbed his chin stubble; he frowned till his face wadded to wrinkles. "Reckon your eldest boy could round them calves to Mayho town for me? A whole day would be saved."

I raised off my chair, hoping. I was nine years old, old enough to go traipsing, to look abroad upon the world.

"Ho, ho," Father chuckled, big to tease, "you wouldn't call that turkey track of a forked road a town. Now, Hazard or Jackson—" he hesitated, seeing Mother's eyes upon him. The posts of his chair sunk level with the floor. "That's a good-sized piece for a boy to walk alone. Thirteen miles, roundy 'bout."

"I'll pay a dollar," Aaron said. "A whole silver dollar. Silas McJunkins's boy will be at my house with the money when they're penned. Silas's boy is driving two cows down from Augland in the morning."

"I saw Mayho on a post-office map once," Father said. "Hit looked to me like a place where three roads butt heads. But if this town soaks hits elbows in Troublesome Creek, hit's bound to be a good 'un."

Mother sent Fern, Zard, and Lark to bed. Before going herself she brought in a washpan and a ball of soap. Father poured hot water from the kettle, and Aaron washed his face and hands, then pulled off his boots and soaked his feet. His feet were blue veined and white, and his heels bore no sign of rust.

"You've got townfolks' feet, all right," Father said. He picked up Aaron's boots, matching them with his own. "They're the difference betwixt a razor and a fro." He grunted in awe. "Man! These boots are bound to make a pinch-knot out o' the frog o' yore foot."

Aaron champed his tobacco cud. "They're right good wearing," he said.

"When I thresh my oats," Father spoke, grinning, "I'm a-liable to buy me a pair."

I SET OFF behind the yearlings with daylight breaking, and before the sun-ball rose I had reached the mouth of Shoal Creek and turned down Troublesome. The yearlings pitted the mud banks with their hoofs, and I sank to the tongues of my brogans. My coffee-sack leggings were splattered; my feet got stone cold. A wintry draft blew, smelling of sap.

The sun-ball rolled up a hill, warming the air, loosening the mud. The yearlings nearly ran my leg bones off. I cut switches keen to whistling; I hollered and hollered, and I stung their behinds. I herded the day long, knowing then how it was to be a cattleman.

Chimney sweeps were funneling the sky when I rounded the yearlings into Aaron Splicer's barn lot. Dark crept into Mayho by three roads, coming to sit among the sixteen homeseats crowding the creek or hanging off the hillsides. I saw Ark, Silas McJunkins's boy, atop a fence post, eating a straw. Though a boy, he was man-tall. His hair shagged over his collar and hid his ears. And he was as muddy as I.

Ark helped pen the calves, and I got a whole look at Mayho town before night blacked everything. A clever place I found it, with Easter flowers blooming on leafless stems in yards, and bare trees growing in rows. One house stood yellow as capping corn, and new-painted. "If I lived in a town," I told Ark, "I'd choose here."

"Mayho's a wart on a hog's nose," Ark said.

"Trees yonder lined up a-purpose. Easter flowers a-blooming the winter."

"I choose woods God planted," Ark said. He raised his arm. "Hit's growing spring. Thar's chimley sweeps raising spit to glue their nests."

We beat on Splicer's kitchen door. Aaron's woman opened it a crack, but we didn't cross the sill, for she saw our muddy clothes and told us to sleep in the barn. She handed us a plate of cold hand-pies, and a rag bag of a quilt. We ate the pies in the barn-loft; we burrowed into the hay, leaving only our heads sticking out.

"A mouse wouldn't raise young 'uns in that trampy quilt," Ark said.

I wondered about my silver dollar. Before going to sleep I asked Ark for it.

Ark swore, "Aaron Splicer never give me a bit o' money. He aims for us to drive steers on Quicksand, and said we're to catch a wagon going that way tomorrow. Claimed he'd pay then, and pay double. Two dollars apiece."

"My poppy'd be scared, me not coming straight home," I complained. "I hain't never been on Quicksand. I oughtn't to go." I felt a grain hurt. "Aaron said he'd send me a dollar. A silver dollar."

"He's not paid me neither," Ark said. "He's got us in a bull hole. I've heared he'd shuck a flea for hits hide and tallow, but he'll bile owl grease ere he pinches a nickel off me."

"I ought to be lighting a rag home," I said.

WE CAME ON Aaron Splicer a quarter-mile up Quicksand at Tom Zeek Duffey's place. He was waiting for us, and had already rounded four prime steers into Tom Zeek's lot.

"I hain't located Crate Thompson," Aaron said, "but I've dis-kivered thar's big beef on this creek, head to the mouth. I'm aiming to get it bought and driv to the railroad siding at Jackson in four days. A four-day round up." And Aaron lifted a foot, pointing at his steers. He kicked the board fence, trying the lot's tightness. "I figure I've put the cat on Crate. These brutes guarantee grease in my skillet." He walked the lot, admiring his cattle.

We looked at Aaron's boots. Tom Zeek and Ark laughed a little. Ark said, "Was he to fall down, he's a-liable to stick one o' them toe p'ints in himself. I'd a'soon wear pitchforks."

"I allow they're tighter than a doorjamb," Tom Zeek chuckled.

"Hain't tighter'n the drawstrings on his money bag," Ark said. "I know that for a fact."

"Dude's his nickname," Tom Zeek told us, "and hit's earnt."

Tom Zeek's woman called us to supper. Not a bite we'd had since the day before, except for a robbing of chestnuts from a squirrel's nest. The table held fourteen kinds of victuals, and Ark and I ate a sight. We drank buttermilk a duck couldn't have paddled, so thick and good it was. We stayed the night, sleeping deep in a feather tick.

The next morning Aaron rousted us before daylight. Tom Zeek Duffey's woman fed us slabs of ham, scrambled guinea eggs, and flour biscuits the size of saucers. We set off, with Aaron ahead. Though willows were reddening and sugar trees swollen with sap, a frozen skim lay on Quicksand Creek and rock ledges were bearded with ice. The sun-ball lifted its great yellow eye, warming and thawing, and by midday a living look had come upon the hills where neither bud nor leaf grew. Icicles plunged from the cliffs. Redbirds whistled for mates.

Aaron bargained and bought the day long. We slept on the puncheon floor of a sawmill near Handshoe that night. For supper and breakfast we ate little fishes out of flat cans Aaron got at a storehouse. We started down-creek again, and where it had taken one day to go up, we spent two gathering the cattle and herding them to Tom Zeek's place. We ran hollering and whooping in the spring air.

We rounded eighteen steers and seven heifers into Tom Zeek Duffey's lot. Tom Zeek told us Crate Thompson had come into Quicksand country and was putting up at John Adair's, a mile over the ridge. "Hit might' nigh cankered his liver when he heard Aaron had beat him to the taw," Tom Zeek said. "Oh, I reckon he started soon enough, but he hain't got a pair o' seven-mile boots like Aaron's." He winked dryly at me and Ark.

Tom Zeek Duffey's lot was packed with steers and heifers, being littler than most folks' lots. Aaron drove extra nails in the board fence; he stretched a barbed wire along the posttops; and he sent for Tom Zeek's son-in-law to come and help him drive the herd into Jackson the next morning. "I wouldn't trust this pen more'n one night," Aaron said. "Hit's too small and rimwrecked."

"Why'n't you take these boys on to Jackson?" Tom Zeek asked. "They'll want to spend the money they've earnt."

I said, "They's something I'm half a-mind to buy." Yet I knew two dollars wouldn't be enough; and I knew I ought to be heading home.

"The Devil, no," Aaron grumbled, "I don't trust fences nor chaps. These boys'd scare worse'n muley-cows at the sight o' a train engine. Why, if Ark walked the Jackson streets with that shaggy head, they'd muzzle him for a shep dog."

"I jist like to see boys right-treated," Tom Zeek said.

Ark said, "My hair hain't so long yit you kin step on it with them finicky boots. Anyhow, I reckon hit's pay-time. You promised two dollars apiece."

"I'm a bit short on change," Aaron said, embarrassed for having to speak his stinginess before Tom Zeek. "Cash on the line had to be paid for them cattle."

"I'm a-drawmg me a line. Lay them two dollars down."

"I'm broke tee-total," Aaron said. "Won't have money for settling till them steers are sold. Why, boys, I figgered you'd be tickled and satisfied with a small heifer for pay. I'll pick you one—one betwixt the two of you."

"You'd pick a runt. Anyhow, a heifer wouldn't rattle in my pocket."

"Hit's yearlings or nary a thing."

"God-dog!" Ark swore angrily. "I hope yore whole gang dies o' the holler tail."

Tom Zeek said, "I allus like to see boys right-treated."

Ark walked sullenly behind the barn, and I tagged along. We sat among dead jimson weeds. Ark chewed a tobacco leaf and spat black on the dry stalks. "I'm one feller Aaron Splicer hain't going to skin. I'm a hicker-nut hard to crack. Some witties he might fleece, but not Old Silas McJunkins's boy Arkles."

"He put the cat on Crate Thompson," I said, "He'll brag now he's sicked one on us."

Ark brightened, opening his mouth. The tobacco wad lay dark on his tongue. "Now, I'm a-mind to go talk to Crate. I bet he could trap Aaron. Hit's said Crate Thompson's a sharp 'un." He grinned, blowing the wad against the barn wall hard enough to make it stick; he strode into the barn and fetched out a pair of mule shears.

I cut Ark's hair. I cut the hairs bunched on his neck, the thick brush hiding his ears, the nest of growth on top of his head; I clipped and gaped and banged his head over.

"I feel most nigh naked," Ark said when I'd finished. "Wisht I had me a looking-glass to see."

We went to the spring behind Tom Zeek's house. Ark stared at himself in the water between the butter jars and churns. "Looks to me my fodder's been gethered," he said. He lifted a demijohn of buttermilk and drank it down. I raked a tad of butter from a bowl with my thumb and ate it.

After night fell we climbed the ridge to John Adair's home-place. John and his woman were gone, late-feeding their stock. Crate Thompson sat before a shovel of fire, driving sprigs into a shoe sole. The shoe was a common old anybody's shoe, and not a cattleman's boot. And Crate was hefty as any of Aaron's steers.

"Draw up a chair and squat," Crate said, speaking with tight lips so as not to swallow the sprigs in his mouth. His eyes were intent on Ark's cropped head. Ark sat down, but I remained standing, awkward and restive.

Ark told Crate our trouble. Crate dropped the shoe, listening with a stub finger sunk into the bag of his chin.

"Where's Dude Aaron got them cattle penned?" Crate asked, his words whistling between the sprigs.

"In Tom Zeek Duffey's lot."

Crate spat the sprigs into his hand. Through his gray eyes a body could almost see ideas working in his head. "Well, now," he said slowly, "I can't think o' nothing but a dumb-bull to cuore Dude Aaron."

"Dumb-bull!" Ark cried in awe.

Crate's great chin quivered merrily. "Strip o' cowhide and a holler log and a rosined string's all it takes. But I'll have no hand in it."

"I'll play my own bull-fiddle," Ark bragged happily. "I know how they're made."

"Hit's ag'in' the law," Crate warned.

"Boodle zack!"

"They's fellers roosting in jailhouses for less."

"I'm not aiming to be skint."

"Ah!" Crate sighed, eying Ark's head. "A rare scalping you've had already."

Ark grinned.

"Ah, well," Crate said, breathing satisfaction, "John ought to have an old hide strip hereabouts." He shuffled away to find one.

"I'm scared to do it," I told Ark. "I'm scared to tick-tack."

"We'll have Dude Aaron calling on his Maker," Ark promised.

"I ought to be a-going home," I said.

WE SEARCHED THE pitch dark on the ridge above Tom Zeek Duffey's barn. Ark tapped fallen trees with a stick until he found a hollow log, a log empty as an old goods box, and with a narrow crack in its upper side. A winged thing fluttered out, beating the cold air, lifting. It complained overhead, asking, "*Ou? Ou?*"

"Scritch owl," Ark named.

Ark set to work on the dumb-bull. He drove twentypenny nails at the ends of the crack in the log; he cut notch-holes in the tips of the hide string and stretched it taut over the nailheads. He worked by feel, dark being mighty thick under the roof of tree limbs. Ark had me resin the hide string while he fashioned a bow of a hickory sprout and a twine cord. The dumb-bull was finished.

We perched on the log, waiting for the cattle to settle. We could hear them moving restlessly in the packed lot, though all were swallowed in blackness. We only knew the direction of the house and barn by the noise of the steers.

Ark said, "Aaron's dropped his boots ere now, and I bet the toes stuck up in the floor like jack-knives."

A bird chirped sleepily near us.

"I'm getting chilly," I said. Anxiety burnt cold inside me, cold as foxfire. "We ought to light a smudge."

"No," Ark said. "They'd spot a blaze. I'm jist waiting till them brutes halt their tromp. Hit's best to catch 'em in a nap."

I made talk, hungry for speech. I asked, "What are them towns o' Jackson and Hazard like?" My teeth chattered.

Ark chewed a pinch of bark. "Folks thar a-wearing Sunday breeches on weeky days," he explained. "Folks living so close together they kin shake hands out o' windows if they're of a mind. Humans a-running up and down like anty mars."

"I aim to see them towns some day," I said. "I aim to. Now, I've lived in Houndshell mine camp, yit it wasn't a town for sartin, just houses pitched in a holler."

"I've traveled a sight," Ark bragged. "I reckon I've been nigh to the earth's end. I been to Whitesburg and Campton and Pikeville. I been to Wheelwright and Hyden. Once I went to Glamorgan, in Old Virginia. Hain't that going some'ere?"

I nodded in the dark, thinking of Mayho, thinking of chimney sweeps riding the sky. I thought, "I've already seen Mayho, and I've been on Quicksand Creek. That's far-away traveling." Then we were quiet a long time. I dozed.

A rooster crowed midnight. Ark jumped to his feet. "Hit's time to witch them steers," he said, awaking me. I trembled with dread and cold. I longed to be at home. Ark dragged the hickory bow lightly across the dumb-bull's string, and the sound jumped me full awake. It was like a wildcat's scream, long and blood-clotting and deafening. But that wasn't a circumstance to when Ark bore down. Then it wasn't one lonesome critter; it was a woods-ful, tearing each others' eyeballs out. I reckon that squall hustled three miles.

Ark paused. The timber was alive with varmints. A squirrel tore through the trees squacking. Wings flapped and paws rattled brush heaps. Below, in the lot, the steers bellowed. We could hear them charging the board fence, crazy with fear. They butted their heads in anguish, and the ground rang with the thud of hoofs. Yearlings bawled like lost chaps.

"We're not right-treating Tom Zeek Duffey," I said. "We oughtn't to destroy his fence. Now, his woman fed us good."

"A favor we're doing Tom Zeek," Ark said. "He's needed that old rotten-posted lot cleared. He needs a new 'un." And he sawed the hide string again, cutting it rusty. Goose bumps raised on me. A scream came from that log like something fleeing Torment. We heard the fence give way, the boards trampled, posts broken off. The steers lit out, bellowing and running, up-creek and down, awaking the country.

Lamplight sprang into the windows of Tom Zeek Duffey's house, and a door swung wide and the shape of a man bearing a rifle-gun printed the light. The gun was lifted, steadied, and a spurt of flame leapt thundering. Birdshot rattled winter leaves far below us, spent with distance.

"Aaron Splicer'll shoot a lead mine ere he hits me," Ark said, and he dropped the bow and ran. He melted into the dark.

I ran too, trying to follow; I ran plumb into a tree, and fell stunned upon the ground. My head rang, and sparks leapt before my eyes like lightning bugs. When I got up at last, Ark was out of hearing, and there was no sound anywhere. I crept on my hands and knees for a spell. I walked to the ridgetop, skirting around Tom Zeek Duffey's place, coming down to the creek on the lower side. I crept and walked for hours.

Daylight broke as I reached the creek road. Spring birds were cutting up jack, and the hills were the color of greenback money. And there in the road I found a fat heifer. She made a glad moo and trotted after me. I let her get ahead; I drove her Shoal Creek way. She looked to be sugar in my gourd, and a pair of thorn-toed boots on my feet, just like Aaron's.

Journey to the Forks

"HIT'S A FAR PIECE," Lark said. "I'm afraid we won't make it afore dusty dark." We squatted down in the road and rested on the edge of a clay rut. Lark set his poke on the crust of a nag's track, and I lifted the saddle-bags off my shoulder. The leather was damp underneath.

"We ought ne'er thought to be scholars," Lark said.

The sun-ball had turned over the hill above Riddle Hargin's farm and it was hot in the valley. Grackles walked the top rail of a fence, breathing with open beaks. They halted and looked at us, their legs wide apart and rusty backs arched.

"I knowed you'd get dolesome ere we reached Troublesome Creek," I said. "I knowed it was a-coming."

Lark drew his thin legs together and rested his chin on his knees. "If'n I was growed up to twelve like you," he said, "I'd go along peart. I'd not mind my hand."

"Writing hain't done with your left hand," I said. "It won't be ag'in' you larning."

"I oughtn't to tried busting that dinnymite cap," Lark said. "Hit's a hurting sight to see my left hand with two fingers gone."

"Before long it'll seem plumb natural," I said, "In a leetle spell they'll never give a thought to it."

The grackles called harshly from the rail fence.

"We'd better eat the apples while we're setting," I said. Lark opened the poke holding a Wilburn and a Henry Back. "You take the Wilburn," I told him, for it was the largest. "I choose the Henry Back because it pops when I bite it."

Lark wrapped the damp seeds in a bit of paper torn from the poke. I got up, raising the saddle-bag. The grackles flew lazily off the rails, settling into a linn beside the road, their dark wings brushing the leaves like shadows.

"It's nigh on to six miles to the forks," I said.

Lark asked to carry the saddle-bag a ways, so I might rest. I told him, "This load would break your bones down." I let him carry my brogans though. He tied the strings into a bow and hung them about his neck.

We walked on, stepping among hardened clumps of mud and wheel-brightened rocks. Cow bells clanked in a redbud thicket on the hills, and a calf bellowed. A bird hissed in a persimmon tree. I couldn't see it, but Lark glimpsed its flicking tail feathers.

"A cherrybird's nigh tame as a pet crow," Lark said. "Once I found one setting her some eggs and she never flew away. She was that trusting."

Lark was tiring now. He stumped his sore big toe twice, crying a mite.

"You'll have to stop dragging yore feet or put on shoes," I said.

"My feet would get raw as a beef if'n I wore shoes all the way till dark," Lark complained. "My brogans is full o' pinchers. If'n I had me a drap o' water on my toe, hit would feel a sight better."

Farther on we found a spring drip. Lark held his foot under the cool stream. He wanted to scramble up the bank to find where the water seeped from the ground. "Thar might be a spring lizard sticking hits head out o' the mud," he said. I wouldn't give in to it, so we went on, the sun-ball in our faces, and the road curving beyond sight.

"I've heared tell they do quare things at the fork school," Lark said, "yit I've forgot what it was they done."

"They've got a big bell hung square up on some poles," I said, "and they ring it before they get up o' mornings and when they eat. They got a leetle sheep bell to ring in the schoolhouse before and betwixt books. Dee Finley tuck a month's schooling there, and he told me a passel. Dee says it's a sight on earth the washing and scrubbing and sweeping they do. Says they might' nigh take the hide off o' floors a-washing them so much."

"I bet hit's the truth," Lark said.

"I've heard Mommy say it's not healthy keeping dust breshed in the air, and a-damping floors everyday," I said. "And Dee says they've got a passel o' cows in a barn. They take and wet a broom and scrub every cow before they milk. Dee reckons they'll soon be breshing them cows' teeth."

"I bet hit's the truth," Lark said.

"All that messing around don't hurt them cows none. They get so much milk everybody has a God's plenty."

The sun-ball dropped behind the beech woods on the ridge. It grew cooler. We rested again in a horsemint patch, Lark spitting on his big toe, easing the pain. Lark said, "I ought ne'er thought to be a scholar."

"They never was a puore scholar amongst all our folks," I recalled. "Never a one went all the way through the books and come out yon side. I've got a notion doing it."

"Hit'd take a right smart spell," Lark said.

We were ready to go on when a sound of hoofs came up the valley. They were far off and dull. We waited, resting this bit longer. A bright-faced nag rounded the creek curve, lifting hoofs carefully along the wheel tracks. Cain Griggs was in the saddle, riding with his feet out of the stirrups, for his legs were too long to fit. He halted beside us, looking down where we sat. We stood up, shifting our feet.

"I reckon yore pappy's sending his young 'uns down to the forks school,"Cain guessed. "Going down to stay awhile and git a mess o' fool notions."

"Poppy never sent us," I said, "We made our own minds."

Cain lifted his hat and scratched his head. "I never put much store by all them fotched-on teachings, a-larning quare onnatural things, not a grain o' good on the Lord's creation."

"Hain't nothing wrong with larning to cipher and read writing," I said. "None I ever heard tell of."

"I've heared they teach the earth is round," Cain said, "and that goes ag'in' Scripture. The Book says plime-blank hit's got four corners. Whoever seed a ball have a corner?"

Cain patted his nag and scowled. His voice rose. "They's a powerful mess o' fancy foolishness they teach a chap these days, a-pouring in till they got no more jedgment than a granny hatchet, a-grinding their brains away with book reading. I allus said, a leetle larning's a good thing, sharpening the mind like a sawblade, but too much knocks the edge off o' the p'ints, and darks a feller's reckoning."

Lark's mouth opened. He shook his head, agreeing.

"Hain't everybody knows what to swallow, and what to spit out," Cain warned. "Now, if I was you, young and tenderminded, I'd play hardhead down at the forks, and let nothing but truth git through my skull. Hit takes a heap o' knocking to git a thing proper anyhow, and the harder hit's beat in, the longer hit's liable to stay. I figure the Lord put our brains in a bone box to sort o' keep the devilment strained out."

Cain clucked his nag. She started off, lifting her long chin as the bits tightened in her mouth. Cain called back to us, but his words were lost under the rattle of hoofs.

"I bet what that feller says is the plime-blank gospel," Lark said, looking after the disappearing nag. "I'm scared I can't tell what is truth and what hain't. If'n I was growed up to twelve like you, I'd know. I'm afeared I'll swallow a lie-tale."

"Cain Griggs don't know square to the end o' everything," I said.

We went on. The sun-ball reddened, mellowing the sky. Lark trudged beside me, holding to a strap of the saddle-bag, barely lifting his feet above the ruts. His teeth were set against his lower lip, his eyes downcast.

"I knowed you'd get dolesome," I said.

Martins flew the valley after the sun was gone, fluttering sharp wings, slicing the air. A whip-poor-will called. Shadows thickened in the laurel patches.

We came upon the forks in early evening and looked down upon the school from the ridge. Lights were bright in the windows, though shapes of houses were lost against the hills. We rested, listening. No sound came out of all the strange place where the lights were, unblinking and cold.

I stood up, lifting the saddle-bag once more. Lark arose too, hesitating, dreading the last steps.

"I ought ne'er thought to be a scholar," Lark said. His voice was small and tight, and the words trembled on his tongue. He caught hold of my hand, and I felt the blunt edge of his palm where the fingers were gone. We started down the ridge, picking our way through stony dark.

II

Down-Creek

Brother to Methuselum

WE'RE NIGH all kinfolks on Green Willow Creek. We jist sort o' marry amongst ourselves, and go our own ways, and don't try to imp the world. Let one o' us get twenty or thirty years growing, let us whoop the Devil down in our blood, and we're liable to stay on this old earth-ball a long time. We're liable to out-live John Shell in the almanac; we're pretty shore to get rotten-ripe before we die. There's been two or three on Green Willow who got so old their faces drawed like mares' noses. But never a one started living square over again after they'd passed beyond a hundred like Uncle Mize Hardbarley. He started from scratch and raised a new set o' teeth. His chin got fuzzy as a freestone peach.

Uncle Mize was a hundred and three when he begun sprouting that second set o' teeth. They was the rail thing, no store-boughten about it. Aye gonnies, it was hard to believe unless you took a look for yourself. Spying into his mouth was like glimpsing a holler stump nested with cowbird eggs. There squatted the grinders, eyetooth and 'cisors, and milk white and pretty as a weaning calf's. Now, Uncle Mize was good tickled. He could stop gumming his tobacco and start chawing.

The next thing I know hairs had took a notion to grow on Uncle Mize's bald head, springing thick as fiddlers in Hell; and Uncle Mize got to jumping around to beat crickets. He throwed his specks away. He never peered through them eye-windows nohow. They'd sot on his nose end, and he only spied through to see the black o' his coffee, or how times stood inside his snapping pocketbook. He put his walking-stick by, and I'm a doodlebug's daddy if he didn't look odd, me never remembering him withouten that stick, and it with a sarpent carved on—a rattlesnake with a mess o' puore-life rattles.

Onnatural it was bound to be, Uncle Mize getting young again, and the Hardbarley family graveyard buried up with folks not nigh so old. He'd dug graves for two wives; nine chaps waited Jedgment. Why, the last one o' his family had gone to Glory except two sons, Broadus and Kell. But Uncle Mize took the fresh start like a sheep takes to March grass, gammicking o'er his farm, worrying a crap in, cussing and bossing. Broadus and Kell hadn't cleared a new-ground in fifteen craps, them being lazy as tarrapins. Pawpaws and sassafras had a deed to the land. Even crows got starved out. Now, by grabbies, they had to raise their backsides and set their shanks to the furrows.

Broadus and Kell was sixty years old, and single. But, Hell's bangers! I don't reckon they could be blamed for not getting dough-beaters when not a woman in Knott County would cross their tracks. They was twins, and as much alike as two whiteoak hoe-handles, and long and tall and stringy, a little humpbacked, and I reckon as common looking in the face as God ever made and let live. Maw vowed they put her in mind o' two granny hatchets grubbing a rotten log, beetle-eyed and nit-brained. Living scarecrows, Maw named them. I don't figure even a grass widow ever sparked airy a one o' them. They was willing all right, willing as hound dogs in 'simmon time, but they never got nowhere.

Maw and all the womenfolks on our creek liked Uncle Mize a heap better than they did his sons, yet Uncle Mize got coalrakings a-plenty. They low-rated him partly because he didn't belong to the church, and never pulled his face down long as a mule's collar on Sunday. He'd go to the church-house though; he'd go and set under the cedars outside. If the preacher stepped on a feller's toes, he could steal out and jaw with Uncle Mize; he could jist forget Eternal Damnation, and fill his chest full o' minty air blowing across Green Willow that hadn't been breathed three times over. Oh, he'd begin to feel content to wring a bit o' rest and pleasure from this life and to let the next 'un rack its own jennies.

I used to hang around Uncle Mize myself. You know how a seventeen-year-old boy is, reckless and onreckoning, big ears and small gumption. Them days I liked talk with seasoning. Uncle Mize could do some o' the finest cussing ever I did hear, slicking the words around his tobacco cud, pouring on the vinegar like nobody this side o' the Hot Place. He could split frog hairs with words. And Uncle Mize was free-hearted, free as weather. I've borrowed his jackknife many the time, and I'd swear every tree on the meeting-ground has got my name whacked in the bark. He carried that knife in his snapping pocketbook and sometimes I found a dime stuck betwixt the blades. I borrowed it every chance I got, I tell you. A money dime would buy a half plug o' fact'ry tobacco. I never did favor home-cuored leaf, which was going catty-corner to my raising, I reckon.

After Uncle Mize's teeth and hair begun growing, it got where he stopped by our place more'n usual. I tell you he was proud o' them grinders and hairs. Maw said to his back that he was the Devil incarnate, horns, hoof, and fork-tail; but once she talked to his face when he throwed off on Pap's bald head. Uncle Mize had said that Pap could shine a fox's eyes with his headtop. Pap grinned, knowing it was gospel, but Maw got madder'n ganders.

"Hit's onearthly for a body to git young ag'in atter they've been old," Maw said. "Hit's ag'in' prophecy. I've seed a plum a-blooming in a January thaw, but nary a one yet but what got a frost."

Uncle Mize figured everybody was jealous.

They was getting scared he wasn't mortal. He didn't think it an accident, him growing young again. "I allus aimed to keep breathing a long time and lived according," he'd say. "I 'stilled my own likker, and raised my own bread and tobacco. I never swallowed a grain o' pizen from a doctor's kitbag. Herbs I fotched out o' the hills and brewed my own cuores. I reckon I'm gitting to be the oldest man in Kentuck.' By juckers, if I don't believe I'm a brother to Methuselum."

Menfolks teased Uncle Mize, but nary a thing they made off o' him. He was foxy as the next 'un, I tell you. They'd ask if he was getting young all over, or was it jist in spots.

"Aye, God," Uncle Mize would brag, "I'm a hickory sapling sprouting out o' leaf mold. Why, I might raise me another family afore thar's singing on the p'int."

Uncle Mize kept the buck passing, not letting it stick on him, though square down inside he must a-known he couldn't live a passel o'years; he must a-realized he'd jumped the season, like Maw said. Yet he never let on. Now, no, they made nothing off o' Uncle Mize. You can't tease and cut a rusty with a man who's laughing bigger'n you are. It's like spitting into Green Willow Creek. You can't hit a fish's eye that way.

I recollect Uncle Mize got a mort o' crap work started that spring, by one hooker m'crook or another. He leapt in behind Broadus and Kell, getting eleven acres o' new ground seeded in corn, and a garden patch planted. But persuading that Broadus and Kell to work reg'lar was like whooping snakes. Allus, Kell hunted a shady spot to stretch his carcass. Broadus haunted the county seat. He could unkiver more reasons for going than a pretty girl's got excuses. He went to see womenfolks come riding side-saddle into town, and he might's well not made knuckle bones about it. Oh, he'd passed sixty years, still he'd never give up hunting a dough-beater. I reckon a man-person is hammered together that way. So it was one-horse work Uncle Mize coaxed and begged and bled out o' his sons. Toward the tag end o' May he had to hire me to pitch in and help.

Broadus and Kell set off one morning for the high swag to stir a corn field. I stayed behind to help Uncle Mize plant a late patch o' Kentucky Wonders yon side the barn. Me and Uncle Mize got through in an hour and lit toward the swag, packing hoes across our shoulders. We climbed a log-snaking path, going nigh straight up. By grabs, it was a pull mounting that hill. Uncle Mize made it handy as I did. We rested on poplar stumps at the top and gazed below at corn growing black-green and bonny as ever I did see. A wind freshet lazed, smelling of tansy, rustling the blades, feeling as good to me as a back scratching. I diskivered two crows flopping overhead, and I reckon they was trying to believe their eyeballs, seeing a fourteen-in-the-family crap at the Hardbarleys,' the first since they'd hatched green eggs. Uncle Mize shore had enough raising to see Christmas with.

"Be dom," Uncle Mize said, squinting at them crowbirds, "I'd have a right clever farm if hit wasn't setting on one edge."

We drapped into the swag through a redbud thicket, meeting the corn at the bottomside of the patch. Broadus and Kell wasn't in sight. The mule had dragged the plow across the field, and stood biting tops. Uncle Mize's anger begun to rise. He horned two hands and bellowed at the mule, his voice mean as a dumb-bull fiddle. The mule jerked his neck and stopped chewing; he blew a peck o' slobber. Uncle Mize cupped his ears. A belch, hard and sour, come from somewheres. He grabbed a sassafras root and tickle-toed to a wahoo tree.

Broadus and Kell lay behind a log in wahoo shade, drunk as sluts on backings. A fruit jar set betwixt 'em. Kell slept peaceful, and Broadus was busy picking anty mars and starting them down Kell's neck. It was a sight, I tell you.

Broadus beaded an eye on Uncle Mize, lifting the jar. "Take a leetle sup, Pap," he said, "and warm up them new teeth."

Uncle Mize swung the sassafras. It whistled a-coming, breaking the jar to smidgens. Broadus jumped to his feet, aiming to high-tail, but Uncle Mize jist brought that sassafras root flat against his noggin, and it wasn't no pulled lick neither. Broadus laid over, cold as clabber. I reckon Kell must o' dreamt there was a war started for he staggered up and swung his arms, asking, "What you gitting so damn brigetty about, Pap?" Uncle Mize jist told him off with that root, and Kell bent low, swearing to beat white-hot horseshoes.

Uncle Mize untwisted the mule's harness; he started along them corn rows, busting middles, geeing and hawing. He had the patch plowed by dinner time, but he sweated and snorted worse'n the mule. I seed he was trembly; I seed the wings of his nose was pale. Oh, that hurt him a heap. I don't reckon he ever got plumb over it.

Uncle Mize took the punies. He moseyed about the house, satisfied to do a bit o' setting. He wasn't so branfired feisty after that crazy plowing. He'd holler to folks traveling Green Willow, begging them to come in and talk. Uncle Mize allus would rather jaw than eat 'lassy foam in October. Bot Shedders oft stopped his mail hack and argued with Uncle Mize. They'd heave and set by the hour. Bot was a lot o' company, I reckon, with me in the fields slaying weeds, and Broadus and Kell piddling. That Broadus and Kell! If there was a shady row, it'd take them a half day to hoe it.

Well, we'd go in for dinner and find Bot running off at the mouth, telling some winding lie that'd red a Frankfort lawyer's face. I wouldn't believe Bot Shedders and him on a steeple o' Bible-books. Bot would stay till dinner time, allus, and I'll be dadburned if he wasn't a bigger eater than a liar. I've seed him down a half gallon o' buttermilk, a full bowl o' shuck beans, two 'tater onions, and a pone o' cornbread at one meal. And the way he went at it, you couldn't eat for looking. I tell you, it was a sight to watch that Bot set down to victuals.

One day I heared Bot tell Uncle Mize something, offhandedly. Bot said, "Uncle Mizey, you ought to git you a woman to pretty up this place. If I was single, and gitting young ag'in, that's plime-blank what I'd do."

"Like a prong-horned billy goat you would!" Uncle Mize snorted, spitting clear across the porch into a bubby bush.

Bot pulled a dry face. "A feller needs him a woman to trim the hairs out o' his ears, and sort o' keep his toenails whacked blunt."

"Ruther to have a good hound dog," Uncle Mize said. "I'm a-liable to take to fox-hunting."

Bot grunted. "To be expected a man'd lose his nerve when he gits beyon' a hundred. Hit must make a passel o' difference. I reckon he jist sort o' crosses the river."

Uncle Mize looked peaked, but he never turned a hair. "That hain't for another to say," he spoke. "I'm the only man ever got to be a hundred and three in Knott County. You wouldn't have no way o' knowing."

"Oh, I was jist figuring," Bot said. "I figure the rocking chair's done got you."

"I got as much spirit as airy a man on Green Willow," Uncle Mize vowed, "yet women hain't running in droves who wants to marry the oldest man this side o' Genesis."

"You can allus git one out o' the paper," Bot said. "If you've got a mite o' property and money, it'll fotch 'em like buzzards to a dead varmint."

"I never heared tell o' such a paper."

" 'Pon my honor, they's a paper a woman can be ordered out of."

Bot's belly got to shaking, but he kept his face sober as a coroner's.

Uncle Mize took a fresh tobacco chaw. "I hain't got no mind for a catalogue woman. Yet, by grabbies, I shore would like to fotch on wives for my two sons. Aye, God, I would."

After that Bot Shedders handled things to suit his own notions, without saying chicken-butter to anybody. He kept stopping every day, and when I'd come in he'd be jawing. And got to where he'd laugh at nothing a'tall. A spell passed before we caught on. One day when I come out o' the field there set Bot with a mess o' letters. I never seed so many letters. There must o' been a dozen. He said they was all Uncle Mize's. But writing was hen tracks to Uncle Mize, and he hadn't cracked a one.

"Who you figure writ them?" Uncle Mize asked.

"Why, Uncle Mizey," Bot explained, "them's women wanting to marry. All you got to do is pick one that suits yore notion."

Uncle Mize cut his eyes at Bot. "How'd them womenfolks know I wanted a wife?"

"I put yore name in the paper. Jist you looky here." Bot fetched a wrinkled newspaper from his jump-jacket pocket, and read some print aloud. "Hit says, 'Oldest Man in Kentucky Seeks Wife.' "

"Read some o' that scratching."

Bot ripped the lid off a letter, reading it to himself. He got to laughing, gagging like a cow with a cob in her throat. He forgot to spit, and his mouth filled with ambeer and dribbled.

"Reading must be a sight o' trouble," Uncle Mize grumbled. "Hit's taking a long dry spell."

"This one's from Georgia," Bot cackled. "Says she's seventy-two, hain't got dyed hair, and keeps a clean house. Says she wants to spend her days o' grace with a mate."

"She sounds right peart," Uncle Mize allowed, "but she's gitting along in years. A woman ripes quicker'n a man."

"Ah," Bot chuckled, "if it's a young 'un you want, maybe she's somewheres." He ripped open more letters, glimpsing at the pages, saying at last, "Here's a girl from North C'lina who is nineteen. Says she's got a step-paw who whoops her, and she aims to run away from home. Says she allus dreamt o' marrying a mountain man."

"Coon my dogs!" Uncle Mize blurted. "I hain't going to rob no cradles."

Bot wanted to rip a few more, but Uncle Mize claimed he'd heared all the reading a body could stand for one day. "That there last one ought to have a taste o' rawhide," he said. "I don't reckon I'll marry a'tall, and they don't seem to be none suiting Broadus and Kell either. Too old or too young, and nary a one middling."

"Broadus wouldn't be so choosy," Bot said. "Anyhow, the letters have jist started coming. You'll git a full pick."

Well, now, that puny spell hung on to Uncle Mize. Oft he'd try a turn in bed. Up and down he was all spring, drinking cherry-bark tea for his blood, reg'lar as he sauced his coffee, and it strong and bitter enough to float an iron wedge. He wasn't in pain, jist weak and no 'count. Bot Shedders stopped by on mail days, keeping peg on Uncle Mize's health, and bringing letters. I reckon he was a right smart company.

Oh, I reckon it was tedious for Uncle Mize when Bot wasn't there, and me and Broadus and Kell in the fields; or me in the field working by my lone, Kell asleep under a shady bush, and Broadus at the county seat. Time can hang heavy as a steelyard pea. Flat o' his back, I reckon a feller can count a lot o' moons on his fingernails, reckon he can do a sight o' clear thinking. It might have helped Uncle Mize take a fancy to one o' them letters. For days hand-running, when Bot come, Uncle Mize would say, "Bottle, read that 'ere letter ag'in," and Bot knew which one. He'd read it willing.

"Hit says her name's Olander Spence," Bot said. "She lives in Perry County, not more'n twenty miles from this creek. Says she's thirty-five and tuck care o' her pappy till he died. Says she washes clothes so clean you'd swear dogwoods bloomed around the house on Mondays. Says she can trash air' man ever she did see hoeing a corn row."

That letter pleased Uncle Mize. It done him better'n cherry-bark tea. One day he said, "I've come on an idea I need a woman fiddling around the house and waiting on me. Hit gits lonesome. Why, that Perry County woman sounds clever. I'm a-mind to fotch her on and marry her."

Uncle Mize allus took notions like lightning takes to a fence post. He clem out o' bed and set to making his plans. If he hadn't been so plagued, by grabs if he wouldn't have mounted a beast and gone after Olander Spence himself. And if the corn and garden hadn't been dovetailing weeds, he'd have sent me. I didn't want to go. Broadus and Kell swore and be-damned if they would. Broadus said, "Hain't my wedding nor funeral. I might fotch a woman for myself, but I'll do no wife-hauling for another." Kell put his number eleven brogans down flat. "I'm sot," he vowed. "I hain't moving."

Either Broadus or Kell plime-blank had to travel. Uncle Mize swore their breeches wouldn't hold shucks if they didn't make up their minds. Finally, he drawed a line in the yard and set them playing crack-o-loo. He fished two silver dollars out o' his snapping pocketbook for pitching. "Fartherest one from the line goes to Perry County," he said, "and he can keep the dollar."

Broadus pitched, coming pretty close to the mark. Kell took a hair aim, aiming like measuring death, and beat him; he made the old plu'bns unum eagle straddle the line. Broadus let in cussing, but he started getting his readies on. Uncle Mize jumped lively, fixing the saddle-bags and bridling two horses. Broadus set off, letting the horses have their own heads and take their own sweet time.

It was on a Tuesday that Broadus headed for Perry County, and if he'd got back the next day there'd been an infare in the week-middle. A forty-mile trip is easy two-day horsebacking. Kell fotched marrying license from the county seat, and Preacher Shade Monrow come to do the hitching, and along traipsed 'Lihu Allison. Where you see 'Lihu, you see his fiddle box, and him itching to play. Now, Bot Shedders had spread the word all right. Folks drained out o' every creek and holler in walking distance; everybody on Green Willow come, except Maw. Why, even a passel traveled from Troublesome Creek, up Shoal, and over the Gap to Green Willow.

But Broadus didn't get back. I hadn't figured he'd make beelines nor crow-flies, not since he'd gone against his own swearing. Broadus's head was hard as an oak burr. Folks waited, the day stretched, and yet no Broadus. I kept thinking o' the corn drowning in grass and weeds, thinking o' the Kentucky Wonder patch a hoe'd never tipped. Afternoon come, and calves begun to bawl. The sun-ball drapped, and folks had to go home disappointed.

I didn't get my natural sleep that night. Uncle Mize sprung a pain in his chest, and I had to set up with him. I wropped a hot rock to lay on his heart; I biled coffee so strong a body could o' walked it; I kept fotching well water. He eased as daylight cracked, and ere I'd struck a nap for myself, aye gonnies, if folks didn't start coming back. O'ernight the word had caught worse'n grippe. Folks traipsed from Rockhouse Creek o' Letcher County, from Dead Mare Branch in the far corner of Knott, from Floyd County and Leslie. Roundabout nigh, everybody come, even Maw. Maw's curiosity got bigger'n her religion. People wadded the yard so thick weeds led a hard life. I thought it a pity a few couldn't be tromped amongst the corn and Wonder beans.

Uncle Mize ate common at breakfast: two hoe cakes, butter and molasses, a middling-sized slice o' ham. Then he went onto the porch and people crowded to shake his hand, the men laughing fit to bust and the women giggling behind handkerchers. 'Lihu whooped his fiddle into "Old Joe Clark" and Uncle Mize cut three steps rusty to prove how limber he was. I knowed Uncle Mize wasn't up to scratch. His face was pale as winter butter. After he'd wrung a peck o' hands he told me he aimed to go back inside and rest a spell, and for me to roust him the first sight I had o' Broadus.

Along nigh ten o'clock I happed to glance toward the creek bend, and there did come Broadus. You couldn't hear the horses' feet clop for all the talking. Folks hung o'er the fence, they stood on tipple-toes, they stretched their necks. There rode Broadus, yet one horse wore an empty saddle. I squinched my eyes, and I saw a woman setting behind Broadus, riding side-saddle.

Bot Shedders saw the same I did. Bot said, "That other nag must o' went lame or throwed a shoe. Hain't no feymale ever sot that close to Broadus afore."

I hustled to Uncle Mize's room. The door was shut. I twisted the knob and opened it, hollering a time or two. I heard no answer. A shade hung the window and it was dust dark. I waited till my eyes got acquainted, and saw Uncle Mize flat o' his back on the bed, with his breeches and socks on. I thought to shake him, but I didn't. I couldn't. Not a sound o' breath rustled out o' him. I jist stood there froze a minute, then I skittered off to find Kell. Kell felt like I did, scared and shaky. We took a long solid look, and it was the truth.

"Let's tell Broadus," Kell said. We closed the door, not saying a word to nobody. Broadus had rode in at the wagon gate and was helping Olander Spence to the ground. I saw right then Uncle Mize had made a fair guess. Olander Spence seemed peart as a spring fryer, and her buck teeth were white as roast-ear grains. Her hands were big and thick and used to work.

Broadus unbuckled the saddles and flung them onto the woodpile. He said to that Spence woman, "You set here on the chopblock till I git the horses barned."

We walked to the barn, Broadus, Kell, and me. They opened the stall doors while I clem up into the loft for hay, and when I come down the ladder Kell had told Broadus.

"He jist blowed out like a tallow dip," Kell said.

Broadus leant against the wall, his mouth open.

Kell grumbled, "That fotched-on woman has got us into a puore mess. By jakes, if you don't have to take her back to Perry County the first thing atter the burying."

Broadus shook his burr head. "She hain't going nowheres," he said. "Me and Olander Spence done some marrying yesterday."

Broadus and Kell latched the stall doors and racked the bridles. They went toward the house, and I stood there in a pile o' shucks, trying to think what to do. I didn't want to go back inside that room where Uncle Mize was, I tell you. I felt like cutting down a tree, or splitting a stack o' rails—anything to brush my mind off o' Uncle Mize. I got a goose-neck hoe, and slipped yon side the barn. I hoed out that patch o' Kentucky Wonders by dinner time.

Snail Pie

THOUGH MOTHER'S face was pale with anger, she didn't speak until Grandpaw Splicer and Leaf and I pushed back our plates. Grandpaw went to the barn to light his pipe, and Leaf followed to ask more about the rattlesnake steak Grandpaw claimed he ate once. I crawled under the house, squatting beneath the kitchen floor, listening. I had a mind to learn whether Father was going to tell of catching me chewing a wad of Old Nine. Mother was set as a wedge against tobacco. She wouldn't spare the limber-jim. I heard her heel strike the floor impatiently; I heard the rounds of Father's chair groan in the peg holes.

"Your step-paw's got to hush his lie-tales at the table," Mother said, her voice pitching high in her nose. "Since he's come to Mayho a meal's victuals haven't rested easy in my stomach. We ought to send him back to that county farm down in the Bluegrass."

"Forty years a drummer," Father said, "forty years of drumming mountain counties. He's too old to change his way." The leather of Father's cattle boots creaked. "Without a line o' big-eyed lies he couldn't have sold gnat balls and devil's snuff boxes. That's what he vows peddling. He's allus been a big hand to tease, and means no harm earthy."

"Every time he sticks his feet under the table it's pickled ants or fried snails. The name of snails I never could stand. Why, my innards turn at the word. And that pipe, foul as a pig pen. I told him straight off a whiff of tobacco sickened me. I warned him to keep it outside the house."

"Paw's a right smart company for the boys," Father said. He had saucered his coffee and was blowing across it. "Keeps them from underfoot; and it's got where I can go bird-hunting without them whining to track along. Oh, we oughtn't to work a hardship on the old man."

Mother's voice dropped from anger to dull complaint. "Old and doty and childish, worse'n any chap. Why, he might even teach the boys to smoke tobacco. I'm bound they'll not get the habit. I can't get Todd to say what he talks about to them, but Leaf did once. He told an awful thing about a mole."

"Oh, I figure he keeps a good eye on the chaps. You'd not know they're wormy if Paw hadn't found out. He offered to roust some boneset leaves to rid 'em."

"I'm no witch to begin brewing herb tea," Mother said. "You buy a bottle of vermifuge."

"Come spring," Father said, "Paw can hoe the garden. Nothing will fight weeds like an old man. I thought I'd pay him a mite to keep him in heart."

"We promised to try him for one month," Mother said. "One month, and not a day beyond." Her words were cold and level. "Three weeks he's been here, and it's moles, slugs, or fish bait three times a day. I say you've got to speak to him. He'll quieten or go back to that county farm. The next time he mentions snails——"

Father clapped his empty saucer against the table-top. "You oughtn't to be so finicky," he blurted. He shoved his chair back and got up. I heard dishes clink fit to break. "I hate like rip to call the old man down. I hate to."

"If you'd heard what he told Leaf," Mother quarreled, her voice rising, for Father's hand was twisting the door knob. "If you'd heard!"

Father slammed the door so fiercely the skillets rattled behind the stove.

I hurried from under the house and ran to the barn. Leaf stalked the calf lot on johnny-walkers Grandpaw Splicer had chopped for him. Grandpaw sat in the crib whittling a cob, and smoking and chewing. He was shaping a new pipe bowl with his barlow knife.

"Grandpaw," I said, "you never did tell me about that mole."

Grandpaw Splicer's eyes rounded, questioning. "Mole?" he asked.

"You told Leaf," I reminded, acting slighted.

"Ah, yes," Grandpaw said, "what some fellers done with a mole varmint." He blew a tobacco cud out of his mouth onto a shuck. He knocked pipe ashes into a crack. Then he opened his mouth suddenly, drawing his tongue back. "Be-jibs," he said, "I've lost another tooth." He spied into the shuck, and there it was. He drew the false plate forth into his hand. "I need me a new set o' teeth, but I've got no money. It'd take many a frog skin. Afore long I'll have to gum victuals."

"I heard Pap say he was aiming to pay you a wage," I said. "I did, now."

"Ah," Grandpaw said. The blue flecks in his eyes shone. "Ah!" He pitched the tooth into a bag of seed corn. "Thar's one grain never'll sprout." He began to whack the cob nub. A kink of smoke twisted from his pipe and the crib filled with the mellow smell of tobacco, ripe and sweet and burning.

I watched the shaping of the cob, drawing in deep breaths of burnt tobacco. "Grandpaw," I said, "I'd give a pretty if you was making that 'un for me."

Grandpaw grunted, clicking his teeth plates. "I knowed of a baby once was larnt to smoke in the cradle. Ruther to draw on a pipe than his mammy's breast. Gee-o, if that little 'un didn't grow up six feet two."

"I been smoking a spell," I confessed.

Grandpaw chuckled. "I figured hit was you slobbered on my pipe stem yesterday. That's why I'm whittling this new 'un."

"Be it for me?" I questioned, hoping.

"Now, no," Grandpaw said, "your mommy hates tobacco like the Devil hates Sunday. She'd hustle me back to that county farm 'gin sundown. But if they comes a time you're bound to smoke, jist steal this new 'un. Never wanted another using my reg'lar."

The bowl of the pipe was nearly finished. Only the dried marrow of the cob lacked scraping.

"Grandpaw," I said, "I'm scared you're a-going to be sent back. I heard Mommy a-talking."

"Hark!" Grandpaw said. He put the barlow down slowly. His face clouded with wrinkles and worry. "Was hit that mole tale?"

"Not square all," I said. "Hit, and some more."

The cob rolled to the crib floor. Grandpaw dipped into the seed corn, filling the pan of his hand with grains, lifting, pouring. His lower lip stuck out blue and swollen, the gray bag of his chin quivered. "Todd," he spoke, "you tell me what your mommy said, and I'll chop you a pair o' johnny-walkers."

"I choose that pipe," I bargained.

"Ruther to die than go back," Grandpaw moaned. "Folks thar perished already, jist won't give up and lay down. Coffin boxes waiting in the woodshop. Hit's cruel. Cruel like what fellers done with a mole once." His eyes dampened; his hands shook, scattering the corn. "You know what fellers done? Started a mole in a bull yearling. That bully run a mile, taking on terrible, and fell stone down dead."

"I'll keep that pipe 'tater holed. Nary an eye'll tetch it."

"I long to stay on here."

I peeked through the crib cracks to see that no one was near. Leaf tramped the far side of the lot on his walkers. I told Grandpaw what Mommy had said. He listened, an arm elbow-deep in the corn sack. "Never tell Leaf a grain o' nothing," I warned him at the end. "He's bad to talk. Jist six, and don't know no better. And nary a word o' snails."

"I'll play quiet-Bob," Grandpaw said. "Aye gonnies, I will."

We heard Leaf coming on his johnny-walkers, crockety-crock. He stuck his head in through the door. "Grandpaw," he called, his mouth curling with mischief, "did you ever eat a horse apple?"

ON SATURDAY FATHER went bird-hunting, and there were quails' breasts for dinner, and gravy brown as cracklings. We sat at the table watching Mother cut the breasts in half. She served her plate and passed the dish. Leaf and I had been starved for two days, having taken the vermifuge Thursday and forbidden to eat a bite since. We could hardly wait longer. Our stomachs were empty jugs.

Father grinned at the dish of fried breasts. Four were no larger than a child's fist. His jaws set with pride. He had brought down three birds with one shot, bagged nine altogether; and he had prepared them too, for Mother would never clean a fowl. He glanced at Grandpaw, seeking a good word for his prowess. "Three with one shot," Father bragged. "Three, now."

Grandpaw's teeth clicked. His lower lip puckered, and I knew he'd thought of a thing to tell. He raised grizzly eyebrows, wondering if he dared.

"One plummet, three bobs," Father said. "That's no fish tale." His mouth slacked with hunger. "Ever see such mud-fat ones?"

"Hit was quare how I killed a bob-white once," Grandpaw said. He spoke slowly, picking his words. "Years ago when I lived in the head o' Jumpup Holler I went a-fishing on Shikepoke Creek. Caught so plagued many I had no place a'tall to put 'em. Jist shucked my breeches, tied knots in the leg-ends, and filled 'em topful o' the prettiest redeyes and big-mouths. So many fish I packed, a button popped off, and be-dabs if hit didn't kill a bob-white."

"Sounds like truth to me," Father laughed. He winked at Mother. She had stopped eating, uncertain; then she took a big bite. Mother did mortally like partridges.

Leaf spoke, his mouth full, swallowing. "Grandpaw, where's Jumpup Holler? I be to go thar."

"Ah," Grandpaw said. He poked his lip out so far it seemed bee-stung. "Why, hit's so far backside o' nowhere folks have to use possums for yard dogs and owls for roosters."

"I bet that hain't the truth," Leaf said.

"Swear to my thumb to my dum," Grandpaw said.

"I know me a tale and hit shore happened," Leaf said. The spark of his eyes lit. He glanced at me and Grandpaw. I got a grain fidgety. Leaf was bad to tittle-tattle.

"Truth?" Mother asked doubtfully. "Truth will keep without salt. Rest your tongue." And she served her plate again.

"Ah," Grandpaw said, thinking back into his head for another tale. "It wasn't allus good times in Jumpup Holler. Once a hard winter come. Ninety days snowfall, ninety days stripping zero. Well, now, I give out o' bread and I give out o' meat. Not a lick o' sweetening in the 'lassy barrel. Not a speck o' nothing to eat the size o' the chinebone of a gnat."

Mother laid her fork by uneasily, waiting. Her mouth was full, but she didn't swallow. I tried to catch Grandpaw's eye. He paid me no mind. He lifted a hand, laying off this story-piece. I tried to poke him with a foot under the table.

"Well, now," Grandpaw went on, "I got my old hog-rifle and searched the woods over. Not a sight o' beast or varmint I had. Then I looked into the sky roof, and by jukes if thar wasn't a buzzard flying. I took a hair aim, fetched him down at one crack, and 'gin to rip the feathers."

Father opened his mouth to laugh, but Mother stared angrily at him. She had paled; her lips were tight against her teeth. Father made a breathy gulp. I slid low in my chair and kicked Grandpaw's knee. He grunted. He glanced at me in a way to tell me he was being careful.

"Did you cook that thar buzzard?" Leaf asked.

"Now, no," Grandpaw replied. "I gethered the hungry smell out o' the meat box, mixed it with frost bite, and fried it with a smidgen o' axle grease. Hit made good victuals too."

Mother swallowed at last. She stared into her plate at a baby partridge's breast. I felt better, though I wished Grandpaw had played quiet-Bob as he'd promised.

"I know me a tale," Leaf said, "and hit's truth. I be to tell."

"Truth?" Mother asked sharply.

"Gourd-head and tell," Father joked. I could see he was glad Grandpaw hadn't eaten that buzzard.

"Be sure it's truth," Mother warned, her voice pitching high and thin. "We could do with a dust of honesty."

Grandpaw lifted his chin. He was a bit anxious.

"Hit was this morning," Leaf began. "That thar worm medicine was retching my innards."

Mother grasped the tabletop. Her knuckles grew white and bloodless; her face turned the color of dough.

"I went running behind the barn," Leaf said, "and thar was Grandpaw Splicer and Todd a-smoking. Todd smoking a cob pipe Grandpaw made for him, a-blowing smoke big as Ike Pike. I be to have me a pipe too."

Grandpaw's chin quivered. His shoulders sagged, and he leaned forward, his eyes watering. Drips ran along the webbed wrinkles of his cheeks. He seemed old, old.

Leaf stared and hushed, suddenly regretting having told. He couldn't think why Grandpaw Splicer wept. His lips trembled. "Grandpaw," he said, trying to patch the hurt, "did you ever eat a snail pie?"

The Moving

WE STOOD by the loaded wagon while Father nailed the windows down and spat into the keyholes to make the locks turn. We waited, restless as the harnessed mare, anxious to hasten beyond staring eyes. Hardstay mine was closed for all time and idle men had gathered to watch us leave. They hung over the fence; they crowded where last year's dogtick stalks clutched their brown leaf-hands into fists.

I saw the boys glance at our windowpanes, their pockets bulging with rocks. I spied into their faces and homesickness grew large inside of me. I hungered for a word, a nod of farewell. But only a witty was sad at my going, only a child of a man who valued strings and tobacco tags, a chap in a man's clothes who was bound forever to speak things backwards. Hig Sommers stood beg-eyed, and fellows were picking at him. One knelt and jerked loose the eel-strings of his brogans.

Though women watched from their porches only a widow-woman came to say a good-by to Mother. Sula Basham came walking, tall as a butterweed, and with a yellow locket swinging her neck like a clock-weight.

Loss Tramble spoke, grinning, "If I had a woman that tall, I'd string her with gourds and use her for a martin pole. I would, now." A dry chuckle rattled in the crowd. Loss stepped back, knowing the muscle frogs of her arms were the size of any man's.

Sula towered over Mother. The locket dropped like a plumb. Mother was barely five feet tall and she had to look upward as into the sky; and her eyes set on the locket, for never had she owned a grain of gold, never a locket, or a ring, or bighead pin. Sula spoke loudly to Mother, glancing at the men with scorn: "You ought to be proud that your man's not satisfied to rot in Hardstay camp, a-setting on his chinebone. Before long all's got to move, all's got to roust or starve. This mine hain't opening ag'in. Hit's too nigh dug out."

The men stirred uneasily. Sill Lovelock lifted his arms, spreading them like a preacher's. "These folks air moving to nowheres," he said. "Thar's no camps along the Kentucky River a-taking on hands; they's no work anywheres. Hit's mortal sin to make gypsies of a family. I say as long's a body has got a roof-tree, let him roost under it."

Men grunted, doddering their heads, and the boys lifted their rock-heavy pockets and sidled toward the wagon. Cece Goodloe snatched Hig Sommers's hat as he passed, clapping it onto his own head. The hat rested upon his ears. The boys placed their hands on the wagon wheels; they fingered the mare's harness; they raised the lid of the tool box to see what was in it. Cece crawled under the wagon, back hound to front hound, shaking the swingletree. I watched out of the tail of my eye, thinking a rusty might be pulled.

Father came into the yard with the key, and now the house was shut against our turning back. I looked at the empty hull of our dwelling; I looked at the lost town, yearning to stay in this place where I was born, among the people I knew. Father lifted the key on a finger. "If a body here would drap this key by the commissary," he said, "I'd be obliged."

Hig Sommers lumbered toward Father, his shirt-tail flying. Someone had shagged his shirt out. "I'll fotch it," Hig cried, stretching both hands for the key as a babe would reach.

"I'm not a-wanting it fotched," Father said. He'd not trust the key to a fellow who wasn't bright. "You've got it back'ards, Hig. I'm wanting it tuck."

Sill Lovelock stepped forward, though he didn't offer to carry the key. "They's Scripture ag'in' a feller hauling off the innocent," he vowed gravely. "I say, stay where there's a floor underfoot and joists overhead."

Father said testily, "There ought to be a statute telling a feller to salt his own steers. Ruther to drown o' sweat hunting for work than die o' dry rot in Hardstay."

Loss Tramble edged near Father, his eyes burning and the corners of his mouth curled. He nodded his head toward Sula Basham. "I'll deliver that key willing if you'll take this beanpole widow-woman along some'eres and git her a man. She's wore the black bonnet long enough."

Laughter sprang forth, gulping in throats, wheezing noses. Sula whirled, her face lit with anger. "If I was a-mind to marry," she said, grudging her words, "it's certain I'd have to go where there's a man fitten. I'd be bound——"

Sill Lovelock broke in, thinking Sula's talk of no account. He asked Father, "What air you to use for bread along the way? There's no manna falling from Heaven this day and time."

Father was grinning at Sula. He saw the muscle knots clench on her arms, and he saw Loss inch away. He turned toward Sill in good humor. "Why, there's a gum o' honey dew on the leaves of a morning. We kin wake early and eat it off."

"The Devil take 'em," Mother said, calming Sula. "Menfolks are heathens. Let them crawl their own dirt." She was studying the locket, studying it to remember, to take away in her mind. I thought of Mother's unpierced ear lobes where never a bob had hung, the worn stems of her fingers never circled by gold, her plain bosom no pin-pretty had ever hooked. She was looking at the locket, not covetously, but in wonder.

"I'll take the key," Sula told Father. "Nobody else seems anxious to neighbor you."

Loss opened his hands, his face as grave as Sill Lovelock's, mocking. He pointed an arm at Sula, the other appealing to the crowd. "I allus did pity a widow-woman," he said. He spanned Sula's height with his eyes. "In this gethering there ought to be one single man willing to marry the Way Up Yonder Woman."

Sula's mouth hardened. "I want none o' your pity pie," she blurted. She took a step toward Loss, the sinews of her long arms quickening. When Loss retreated she turned to Mother, who had just climbed onto the wagon. Sula and Mother were now at an eye level. "You were a help when my chaps died," Sula said. "You were a comfort when my man lay in his box. I hain't forgetting. Wish I had a keepsake to give you, showing I'll allus remember."

"I'll keep you in my head," Mother assured.

"I'll be proud to know it."

We were ready to go. "Climb on, Son," Father called. I swung up from the hindgate to the top of the load. Over the heads of the men I could see the whole of the camp, the shotgun houses in the flat, the smoke rising above the burning gob heaps. The pain of leaving rose in my chest. Father clucked his tongue, and the mare started off. She walked clear out of the wagon shafts. Loose trace chains swung free and pole-ends of the shafts bounded to the ground.

"Whoa ho!" Father shouted, jumping down. A squall of joy sounded behind us. Cece Goodloe had pulled this rusty; he'd done the unfastening. Father smiled while adjusting the harness. Oh, he didn't mind a clever trick. And he sprang back onto the wagon again.

Loss Tramble spooled his hands, calling through them, "If you don't aim to take this widow along, we'll have to marry her to a born fool. We'll have to match her with Hig Sommers."

We drove away, the wheels taking the groove of ruts, the load swaying; we drove away with Sill Lovelock's last warning ringing our ears. "You're making your bed in Hell!" he had shouted. Then it was I saw the gold locket about Mother's neck, beating her bosom like a heart.

I looked back, seeing the first rocks thrown, hearing our windows shatter; I looked back upon the camp as upon the face of the dead. I saw the crowd fall back from Sula Basham, tripping over each other. She had struck Loss Tramble with her fist, and he knelt before her, fearing to rise. And only Hig Sommers was watching us move away. He stood holding up his breeches, for someone had cut his galluses with a knife. He thrust one arm into the air, crying, "Hello, hello!"

The Scrape

I WAS jist reckoning to myself that foxes were traipsing there on Cannel Creek and wishing I had me a pack o' hounds when I come on Jiddy Thornwell stretched in the road where it ducks for a span out o' the bottom. The ivy shade was mighty black, though the moon-ball yallered the creek water and made straw stacks o' trees, but I knew Jiddy the minute my eyes sot on him. I'd a-known him anywheres in this world. When he's drunk he gits loose-j'inted, his arms and legs hanging on like they was sewed.

When first I saw Jiddy, I figured going on to the square dance at Miles Jarrells's like I'd started. A feller bearing a thimble o' sense wouldn't run with Jiddy Thornwell. If ever one was born for Hell, he was it. Oh, bad trouble was laying for him, and I didn't aim to be nigh when it happened. Then I thinks to myself, a body oughtn't to allow even a forked-foot devil to git their necks cracked with a wagon wheel, or their brains stepped in by a nag. He was laying right pretty for one or t'other. And, anyhow, I sort o' figured Jiddy might have a bottle on him and I was beginning to crave a drink. I give him a light kick. He moved a speck, opening his eyes. Now, he wasn't half as drunk as I'd thought.

"Jiddy," I called, "what're you sleeping smackker-dab in the road for?"

He got up, limber and wide awake.

"You've been laying dandy to git yore head spilled," I warned, slapping his hip pocket. I felt no bottle, jist a knife and the little 32-squeeze-trigger he allus carried. He didn't have a gill o' likker. "I've seed fellers drank and still act with sense."

"I hain't drunk," Jiddy said. "Not a bit out o' the way." Then he asked where I was heading.

"You come on along to Miles Jarrells's," I said. "There'll be a crowd o' girls thar, and Cumine most likely, and enough fiddlers to curl the shingles." Now, I knew he'd been sparking Cumine Randle nigh on to a year; and I knew Sam Avery had been cutting in on him lately. Why, even there'd been a time when I was sweet on Cumine myself, but I hadn't a snowball's chance. Allus I've been one willing to swallow a fact when hit's stuck in my throat.

Jiddy shook his head. "I've been a-waiting," he said. "Me and Sam Avery's going to settle our trouble tonight, and I'm aiming for you to be an eyewitness. I aim everything to be done fair and square."

"Where's Sam?" I asked uneasily, knowing Damnation would bile over when they locked horns. Oh, I'd no mind to be there. I begun planning to waggle out some way.

"We've got everything fixed," Jiddy said. "Sam swore he'd be waiting at the creek-mouth when the moon riz. We're going to fight, and the best man gits the right o' way. The nerviest man amongst us kin go right along to Miles Jarrells's with you."

"Jiddy," I blurted, "you're a jug-head witty to dream I'm going to mix in yore scrapes."

"Let's find a drink first," Jiddy said, not offering to argue. "Bill Hopson's got a still yon side the ridge."

"I never liked Bill's snake spit," I said. "His's the sorriest likker ever made on Cannel Creek."

"We hain't got time to cull nothing," Jiddy said, "come backings, singlings, or rotgut."

We skinned up the ridge, through bresh and brier, and come out on top in a patch where the moonlight made blooming dogwoods out o' sarvice bushes. Jiddy told me to stay there till he got back, and he crept off. I heard his brogans squeaking like a nest o' crickets; I heard hounds barking afar, and Shep Hillin's puore-blood bull bellow and blow. A gale-bird sung her a ballad. Hit was a lonesomey place, and I'd have skedaddled if it hadn't been for me wanting a dram so bad my tongue prickled. A fool I was for not high-tailing.

Pretty soon I heard Jiddy's squeeze-trigger fire a couple o' times. I dropped flat to the ground. I didn't hear a thing more till Jiddy's brogans squeaked again. He walked into the clearing.

"What's up?" I choked, picturing Bill Hopson with the moonlight shining through him.

"Come on," Jiddy said. "I jist shot to scare Bill. He tuck down the ridge faster'n a deer."

I recollect Bill Hopson's still was hid clever as ever I did see. We waded bresh, seeing nothing, and of a sudden there it was, under a wedge o' cliff rock. Fire burnt beneath the kettle, yet not a drap o' likker had driddled through the worm.

Jiddy swore a sack o' cuss words. He leant over the tub o' still beer and scooped a gourd dipperful, taking a drink long as London bridge.

"Git away from that stuff," I warned. "Hit's pizen."

Jiddy kept on drinking, and I reckon he downed a pint or more. It made my belly retch to see him. Then finally we lit out again, turning over the backbone o' the hill, meeting Cannel Creek yon side o' Loss Ramsey's homeseat.

A short ways down the road we heard Loss's thumping keg the same as if hit had been setting in the middle o' the road. I told Jiddy to wait this time and rest his bones while I headed up the holler. Loss had a big run on, and looked fidgety when I come along. I told him he'd do well to sew breeches on that thumping keg, else the Law'd be visiting. Loss give me a short quart, to put himself in the clear. It was fresh-run, and warm. I swallowed a gill and stuck the bottle under my shirt and belt. When I got out o' that holler I felt more in a notion o' being at Jarrells's square dance than any time ever.

Jiddy wouldn't hear to me going. "Wait till we git affairs settled," he said. "Jist you wait." And he asked whether I'd got a drink from Loss. I lied like a dog. "Now, no," I said, "not a sup."

O'er rocks and ruts I tromped, following Jiddy. With a dram warming my innards I sort o' forgot about Sam Avery; he slicked plumb off my mind till we reached the creek's mouth and I saw him waiting, as Jiddy'd said he would be. I stepped up to Sam. I said, "Ho, Sam'l," and I lit in telling him the trouble him and Jiddy was headed for. I told him Cumine Randle wouldn't thank nary a one o' them. I talked till my head rattled.

Sam called me a bad name, and I knew, come a thousand years, I couldn't break his notion to fight Jiddy. Allus, I've liked to see a good knock-down and drag-out scrap without guns, brass knucks, or onfairness. Watching fellers crack skulls with bare fists is one sight I pleasure in, yet I'd no mind for Jiddy's and Sam's tear-up. They'd battle till their arms wore to the elbows. Hit was no telling what they'd do to git a clear track with Old Bud Randle's Cumine.

I shut my head and walked a ways; I leant into a willow bush and tuck a drink. Jiddy and Sam sot themselves on a log and begun to figure a plan, talking cool as moss. I heard every word, but my likker busied me and I didn't pay much mind. Anyhow, I was thinking I'd be making rabbit tracks to that square dance soon as I got rested from all the ridge running me and Jiddy'd been doing.

Sam hollered me over to the log and ordered his and Jiddy's arms tied together. He handed me a cut o' plow rope the length of a grown blow adder. Well, I figures, if they fight one-handed, they'll do half the damage. Hit satisfied me. I jist tuck Sam's say-so and latched a knot around his left wrist tight as hickory bark; and Jiddy being left-handed, I tied a skin-peeler to his right wrist. Six inches o' rope hung betwixt them. They had one free hand apiece. Now, I hain't one to meddle, but I spoke up, "You fellers give over yore guns and I won't mind to staying as an eye-witness." And, by gollyards, if they didn't. Jiddy reached me his little squeeze-trigger, and Sam drawed forth an old German Luger—the one he parted Greb Tillett's hair with last August. I laid them both on a rock.

Jiddy told me to treat them to a drink. He knew all the time I had that Loss Ramsey stuff. He jerked the stopper with his teeth, offering the bottle to Sam. Sam tuck a long pull out o' it, and I noted his face was dead white; hit was corpse color, though I'd a-thought he wouldn't a-paled at a hanging, even. I figured it to be a trick o' the moonlight. Jiddy tuck a sup, the leetlest ever I saw him take, and that was fair likker too, even if a character like Loss Ramsey did make it. I stared at Jiddy. Well, there was nothing partic'lar about his face, but his eyes were mighty quare. His eye-spots flicked like a jaybird in a cherry tree. And I recollect he stood loose, his arms and legs seeming pinned on. Bill Hopson's still beer had got him shore.

I was downing a gill when Sam told me to stand clear. I stepped aside, my worry sort o' put by. Then Jiddy told me to git away back. I crawdabbed a dozen yards to a spice bush, and I had jist got settled when I saw Sam's and Jiddy's knives. Oh, I'd plime-blank forgot about knives. Sam and Jiddy snapped the blades open, and stood facing. Them blades flashed blue and sharp and cold. I chilled. I couldn't have moved if the hills had come a-toppling.

Now I've seed two wildcats fight, but it wouldn't hold a tallow dip to this; this was something I hope never to glimpse again if I live to be old as Noah's goose.

I recollect it was Sam who struck first, sort o' swinging his arm out, angling. If there'd been a wind, his knife would o' whistled. I heard a rip like a saw-blade cleaving a pine sapling.

The span of Jiddy's back hindered my sight and I couldn't tell for sartin, but the blade must a-nailed his side. Yet he didn't make a sound. He jist swung his knife as if to cut the key-notch of an oak. I'd vow he split a couple or three o' Sam's ribs. Sam wove, shaking himself, gurgling. He gurgled like water squiggling the ground during a rainy season.

I reckon I was crazy drunk or I'd a-done something. My feet growed roots. My legs were cedar posts withouten a j'int. I begged Sam and Jiddy to quit; I bellowed till I couldn't git a sound out o' my throat. I shet my eyes and fell down crying. Them was the first tears I'd shed since I was a chap and they come hard. They sot my eyeballs on fire.

I cracked my eyelids, spying. I seed Sam and Jiddy laying alongside each other on the ground, laying still as logs. And the first thing I knew I was running down Cannel Creek. I reckon I'd have run till I drapped hadn't it been for my bottle working from under my belt. I grabbed it and threw it twisting. It fell amongst a patch o' rocks ahead and never busted. When I got to it, I captured her again and heeled her up, draining the last drop.

I didn't run any more. I jist walked along peart, thinking o' what Jiddy had said once about wanting to be buried in a chestnut coffin so he'd go through Hell a-popping; and I thought of another thing that burnt in my head. I thought o' sparking Cumine Randle.